Baby Taj

by Tanya Shaffer

A SAMUEL FRENCH ACTING EDITION

SAMUEL FRENCH

FOUNDED 1830

NEW YORK HOLLYWOOD LONDON TORONTO

SAMUELFRENCH.COM

ISBN 978-0-573-69842-2   Printed in U.S.A.   #29211

MUSIC USE NOTE

Licensees are solely responsible for obtaining formal written permission from copyright owners to use copyrighted music in the performance of this play and are strongly cautioned to do so. If no such permission is obtained by the licensee, then the licensee must use only original music that the licensee owns and controls. Licensees are solely responsible and liable for all music clearances and shall indemnify the copyright owners of the play and their licensing agent, Samuel French, Inc., against any costs, expenses, losses and liabilities arising from the use of music by licensees.

IMPORTANT BILLING AND CREDIT REQUIREMENTS

All producers of *BABY TAJ must* give credit to the Author of the Play in all programs distributed in connection with performances of the Play, and in all instances in which the title of the Play appears for the purposes of advertising, publicizing or otherwise exploiting the Play and/or a production. The name of the Author *must* appear on a separate line on which no other name appears, immediately following the title and *must* appear in size of type not less than fifty percent of the size of the title type.

BABY TAJ was first produced by TheatreWorks at the Mountain View Center for the Performing Arts in Mountain View, California, September 28 to October 23, 2005. The performance was directed by Matt August, with sets by Joe Ragey, costumes by Fumiko Bielefeldt, lighting by Pamila Gray, and choreography by Sheetal Gandhi. The cast was as follows:

RACHEL	Lesley Fera
ANJALI	Sunita Param
CHANDRA	Qurrat Ann Kadwani
SUNITA	Kavita Matani
ARUSTU	Indrajit Sarkar
OSHO	Oomung Varma
ABHI	Sam Younis
MRS. SHARMA	Rashmi Rustagi
DANCER	Rachel Rajput
NATHAN/SAM/MIKE	Noel Wood
ENSEMBLE	Anil Margshayam, Janak Ramachandran, Rishi Shukla

CHARACTERS

RACHEL – A 37 year-old Jewish-American woman. Free-spirited travel addict. Single.

ANJALI – Her best friend, an Indian lesbian in her thirties who has lived in the U.S. for at least nine years. Single.

CHANDRA – Arustu's wife. Intelligent and quick-tempered. 30-ish.

SUNITA – A girl in her late teens, servant of the Sharmas.

ARUSTU – Mrs. Sharma's son. An astrologer. 30s. A prankster.

OSHO – Chandra and Arustu's six-year-old son.

MRS. SHARMA – Anjali's grandmother. A stern matriarch from Agra, India. 70's.

ABHI – Arustu's cousin. Teacher of Hindi, student of history, poet. Intellectual. 30s.

NATHAN – A friend of Rachel's. 20s or 30s.

MIKE – A friend of Rachel's. Medical intern. 20s or 30s.

TERI – Mike's wife. Medical intern also. 20s or 30s.

SAM – An ex-boyfriend of Rachel's. Mid-30s.

MOTHER – Abhi's Mother, 50s or 60s

COURTIER, LADY, PRINCE, ARJUMAND, GIRL, MAN, various historical characters who appear only in movement sequences.

AUTHOR'S NOTES

Since *Baby Taj* takes place in multiple locations, I suggest a simple, stylized set of moveable pieces. The back wall may be a cyclorama, so that colors and shapes can be projected onto it as Abhi and Rachel visit the various monuments. The scene shifts should be fluid, with cross-fades rather than blackouts as often as possible.

Multiple-casting can permit as few as seven actors, if desired. (This would involve doubling Anjali/Sunita and Chandra/Mrs. Sharma.) A cast of nine or more actors is preferable.

A NOTE ON PUNCTUATION

Three dots (...) are intended to signal a trailing off inflection.
An em dash (–) is intended to signal an interruption.

To my three boys: David, Tavi ("Daby"), and Elon;
and to Elena and Johnny, with love.

(PROLOGUE: As the house lights fade, gentle music is heard. A woman is seen in silhouette, rocking a baby. Stars are visible above her, as if we are peering down at this little scene from out in space. The following language is heard in voiceover.)

RACHEL. *(voiceover)* I've dreamed you for so long, I can hardly believe you're with me now. Yet here you are: a tiny human voyager, sleeping off the shock of migration. I want to gather up joy and lay it at your feet, to banish grief to an island so remote that it can never find you. Instead I give you this world in all its startling detail. One day you'll ask me how you got here. When you do, I'll tell you this story.

ACT I

Scene One

(Rachel's bedroom. RACHEL is lying on her bed, facing upstage with her head toward the audience. ANJALI is about to inseminate her with a plastic syringe. ANJALI is five months pregnant.)

RACHEL. Wait!

ANJALI. What?

RACHEL. Wait!

ANJALI. Why?

RACHEL. Just…

ANJALI. Do you need to use the bathroom?

RACHEL. No –

ANJALI. Are you cold? I'll turn on the space heater.

RACHEL. No –

ANJALI. Then what? What is it? Rachel, this isn't the time for guessing games. These little nippers only last half an hour once they're thawed.

RACHEL. Nothing.

ANJALI. Good. Now on your back and don't give me any more lip.

RACHEL. It's just –

ANJALI. I said on your back, straight girl. Never cross a lesbian holding a turkey baster. I've got sperm, and I'm not afraid to use it.

RACHEL. (RACHEL *lies down, then pops back up.*) Can't we refreeze it?

ANJALI. You know we can't refreeze it. Half of them will die. *(Pause. Soothingly)* What's the matter, Rache? Are you afraid? I promise it won't hurt. What's that you keep telling people: "quicker than sex, and a lot less messy?" When you injected me I didn't even feel it, remember? I told you to hurry up and you were already done.

RACHEL. It's not that.

ANJALI. Then what?

RACHEL. It's just…

ANJALI. What?

RACHEL. *(breath)* I have to postpone it.

ANJALI. *What?*

RACHEL. *(pulling down dress, sitting up, turning)* Just for, like, a month. I got this amazing assignment. I just found out two hours ago. A once-in-a-lifetime opportunity.

ANJALI. Not again.

RACHEL. To go to India, Anj, and you know how I've been wanting to –

ANJALI. Not now. Not after –

RACHEL. It's for this totally hip new travel site. I'd get to do my favorite kind of writing, all attitudey and bloggy and –

ANJALI. You promised, Rachel. You promised you wouldn't let me do this alone!

RACHEL. I won't! It'll just be –

ANJALI. We made a *pact*.

RACHEL. I know we did! And I'm gonna keep it!

ANJALI. Because I would not have started yet. I would have waited. At least until I finished school, till I had a steady job.

RACHEL. I know –

ANJALI. But you said we'd help each other out. "Carpe diem," you said, "No time like the present."

RACHEL. I just need *one* month, Anj –

ANJALI. A *month?*

RACHEL. Four weeks! And then I'll come back and –

ANJALI. You won't.

RACHEL. What?

ANJALI. You *won't* come back. You'll stay. Like you did in Haiti. Like you did in Senegal. I'll get an e-mail saying that you're extending your trip because National Geographic just *had* to have a piece on the tsunami fallout** or the conflict with Pakistan, or –

RACHEL. That's not fair.

ANJALI. It's not?

RACHEL. This is different. You know it is.

ANJALI. You bet it is – I'm five months pregnant!

RACHEL. Come on. I'm not deserting you. I *want* a baby. You know that. I spent a thousand dollars on sperm, for God's sake!

ANJALI. *(waving vial)* And it's going to waste!

RACHEL. Just that one vial. I'll come back and use the others – I swear I will… *(Pause. Softening, slowing down.)* Come on. I'm not going to bail on you. Not on something as important as this. You're my best friend! We've been roommates for, what, nine years? You

---

*Feel free to update with contemporary reference

know me better than my own mother! Of course that's not saying much…Anyway. Don't worry. This is just a *short trip*. I'll be back in plenty of time to take birth classes with you, and to shop for car seats, and…It's better to space them out a bit anyway, don't you think? How much could I help you when your baby's little if I'm about to pop one out myself?

ANJALI. What if you meet some guy? Then it'll be another six months before you dump *him,* by which time my child will be almost –

RACHEL. *Please.* I'm done with that. I told you. I have dated enough loser jerks for the next three thousand lifetimes. From now on, you can call me Celibate Sue; Celly for short.

(**ANJALI** *gives her a grim look.*)

This'll be a quick job. In and out. I'll be back before you know it. *(pause)* Come on, Anjali. *(Pause. Trying to get her to meet her eyes.)* Anjali?

ANJALI. I'm scared.

RACHEL. I'll be home in plenty of time for the birth.

ANJALI. I'm scared anyway.

RACHEL. I know.

ANJALI. *(Pause. They look at each other. Sighs.)* Where in India will you go?

RACHEL. *(carefully)* That's…another thing I'd like discuss with you.

ANJALI. *(looks at her for a moment, then catches on)* Oh, no. No!

Scene Two

*(One week later. The Sharmas' living room in Agra,
India.* RACHEL *has just arrived.* CHANDRA *carries a
baby.)*

CHANDRA. Welcome to Agra. I am Mrs. Sharma.

RACHEL. Mrs. Sharma! It's a pleasure to – wait, *you're* Mrs.
Sharma?

CHANDRA. Oh no, I see what you are thinking. I am not
Mrs. Vasudhara Sharma! I am Chandra, her daughter-
in-law.

RACHEL. Oh, okay. I thought you looked kind of young to
be Anjali's grandmother!

CHANDRA. *(laughing)* Sit down, please. Just set your things
down anywhere. You must be so tired.

RACHEL. Strangely enough, I feel fine. Somewhere over
Thailand I hit my second wind. *(going gaga over the
baby)* Who's this little cherub?

CHANDRA. This is Sachi.

RACHEL. How old is she?

CHANDRA. Four months.

RACHEL. Oh, what an angel. Look at those eyelashes!

CHANDRA. Yes, everyone remarks on that. Let us hope
her mind will be equally remarkable. *(Pause. Eagerly)*
My mother-in-law tells me you will stay with us for an
entire month.

RACHEL. If it's no trouble.

CHANDRA. Oh no, of course not! We are delighted to have
you. When Anjali first went to school in America, she
used to visit us every year. But since her mother died,
she's stopped coming. Now we have not seen her in
more than six years. Her friends are our only link, and
most of them stay only a day or two. We are just coming
to know them and then *phhht!* they are gone. *(Pause)*
But you must be hungry. Let me serve you some lunch.

RACHEL. I'm fine, thanks.

CHANDRA. It is no trouble.

RACHEL. I –

CHANDRA. *(Overlapping. Shouts.) Sunita! Khana! (to* **RACHEL***)* How will you occupy yourself? There is not much to do in Agra once you have viewed the monuments.

RACHEL. Oh, don't worry about that. I'll talk to people. Gather stories.

CHANDRA. You enjoy history?

RACHEL. I'd better. It's paying for my trip.

CHANDRA. *(not understanding)* It's…

RACHEL. I'm writing a series of articles for an internet site.

CHANDRA. You are a journalist?

RACHEL. *(nods)* Travel writer.

CHANDRA. You have come to the right household. My husband's cousin is very knowledgeable about the history of Agra.

RACHEL. Anjali mentioned him. He's the shy one, right?

CHANDRA. About most things, he says very little. But once you get him started on history, you can never shut him up!

*(***RACHEL*** takes off her jacket or overshirt and crosses to her backpack. She takes out a bandana and pats her face.)*

You are hot? Do you want to bathe? Sunita can prepare a bath for you.

RACHEL. Not right now, thank you.

CHANDRA. Water is refreshing.

RACHEL. Thanks, I'm –

CHANDRA. Yes? *(prepares to call* **SUNITA***)*

RACHEL. No. Later. Thanks.

CHANDRA. *(slightly put out)* Hm. Please, sit down. *(pause)* So how is our Anjali?

RACHEL. *(evasive)* She's fine. Working on her dissertation.

CHANDRA. That girl! She has been a student for nine years. She will be an old woman by the time she finishes!

Who will want to marry her then?

(While **RACHEL** *searches for a response,* **SUNITA** *enters and places the lunch on the table.)*

RACHEL. *(to* **SUNITA***)* Thank you.

*(***SUNITA** *giggles with embarrassment and quickly exits, hiding her face.* **RACHEL** *watches her, slightly perplexed.)*

CHANDRA. Will you take chai?

RACHEL. No thanks, water's fine.

CHANDRA. Please.

RACHEL. *(shrugs)* Okay.

CHANDRA. *(shouts toward kitchen)* Sunita! Chai! *(to* **RACHEL***)* My husband's cousin will accompany you to see the monuments.

RACHEL. Oh that's okay, I enjoy going solo.

CHANDRA. You cannot go alone! There are bad men about who prey on tourists.

RACHEL. Thank you, but I've actually done quite a bit of –

CHANDRA. *(overlapping)* But why do you come in May? The tourists come between October and February. The heat is terrible now. Foreigners cannot bear it.

RACHEL. *(Nods. Sighs.)* Yeah, well, my editor's a bit of a sadist.

CHANDRA. Sadist?

RACHEL. He likes watching people suffer.

CHANDRA. *(with interest)* Really?

RACHEL. Mm hm. Readers like it too. Heat stroke, rashes, dehydration – they eat that stuff up. *(***SACHI** *gurgles. Eagerly)* Can I hold her?

*(***CHANDRA** *hands her the baby. To* **SACHI***.)*

Hi, sweetness. Hi, sugar plum pudding pie. Hi bunny bucket buggy boo. Hi pumpkin dumpling, munchkin bunchkin –

CHANDRA. I take it you are fond of babies.

RACHEL. Can't stand 'em.

CHANDRA. You have your own?

RACHEL. Not yet.

CHANDRA. You are married?

RACHEL. Uh-uh. Nope. Not married.

CHANDRA. How old?

RACHEL. Thirty-seven.

CHANDRA. So old!

> (**SUNITA** *enters.*)

SUNITA. *(shyly)* Chai.

RACHEL. Thank you.

> (**SUNITA** *exits, giggling.* **RACHEL** *gestures after her.*)

What's with her?

CHANDRA. You confuse her with your thanks.

RACHEL. *(shrugs)* She brought the chai…

CHANDRA. It is her job. *(Pause. Definitively.)* It is because of the sex, you know.

RACHEL. Excuse me?

CHANDRA. It is because of the sex that you American girls will not settle down.

RACHEL. I don't –

CHANDRA. Many of Anjali's friends have visited us. All girls older than twenty-five years. None of them married, not one! In this country, you marry one man, you are with him your whole life! He is the only one who will share your bed. He may be a kind man or a bad man, a smart man or a stupid man. No matter. He is your husband, and you will never be rid of him. In your country, you try one, throw him away, get a new one. If he is no good, you throw him away too and find another. It is like eating sweets. Once you have tasted one, you want more and more. Today ice cream, tomorrow halva, the next day kheer. You simply cannot stop.

RACHEL. That's a bit –

CHANDRA. Not true?

RACHEL. I'd like to think it's more complicated than that.

CHANDRA. Tell me, Rachel. Are you a virgin?

RACHEL. That's kind of a personal question.

CHANDRA. Please! You will not shock me. I tell you, I have met many American girls. One girl who was here, Trinity, we became good friends. She had just broken with her boyfriend. They were traveling together, and he left her for another girl. Right here, in my arms, she cried and cried. Oh, how she cried!

RACHEL. Maybe once we get to know each other better –

CHANDRA. Please! We are women! You can speak freely.

RACHEL. *(pause)* Okay. *(slowly)* I know this will sound strange, but in my country, if I were a virgin at my age, people would think there was something wrong with me.

CHANDRA. Really?

(SUNITA *enters, takes* CHANDRA's *cup, exits.*)

Do you have a boyfriend now?

RACHEL. No.

CHANDRA. But you have had one.

RACHEL. Well, yes.

CHANDRA. You have had more than one?

RACHEL. *(uncomfortable)* Sure.

CHANDRA. Two or three?

RACHEL. I… *(laughs nervously)*

CHANDRA. More even than that!

RACHEL. Well…

CHANDRA. Four, maybe.

RACHEL. *(lying)* Yes, about four.

ARUSTU. *(from offstage)* Hello, ladies!

(ARUSTU *enters. Goes to* SACHI.)

Hello my little Sachi tachi bachi.

CHANDRA. Here is my husband.

RACHEL. *(rises, relieved)* Pleased to meet you. I'm Rachel Freed.

(ARUSTU *and* RACHEL *shake hands.*)

ARUSTU. Arustu Sharma. The pleasure is mine.

RACHEL. Aru-stú?

ARUSTU. It is Hindi for Aristotle. Because I am a deep thinker. *(He strikes a thoughtful pose.)*

CHANDRA. Where is the boy?

ARUSTU. The boy? *(gasps)* I must have left him at the petrol station.

CHANDRA. Very humorous. *(to* **RACHEL***)* My husband is the next Govinda.

RACHEL. Govind –

CHANDRA. Our famous comedian.

(**OSHO** *runs in and throws himself on* **CHANDRA***.)*

OSHO. Mummy!

CHANDRA. *(to* **RACHEL***)* My son, Osho. *(to* **OSHO***)* Oh! You are dirty! Go wash your hands, naughty boy! Look what he has done to my kurta!

(**OSHO** *exits.)*

ARUSTU. You are from America?

RACHEL. Yes.

ARUSTU. *(scrutinizing her)* Born when?

RACHEL. Excuse me?

CHANDRA. My husband is a professional astrologer. He wants to know your birth date so he can analyze you.

ARUSTU. But you must be tired. Is my wife wearing you out with her questions?

CHANDRA. We were having a very nice conversation until you disturbed us.

ARUSTU. Chandra will ask questions all day and all night if you permit it. She is a very curious person.

CHANDRA. Ha! It is my husband who is curious. He will drag you away from me so that he may question you himself.

ARUSTU. *Cha,* Chandra! Let the girl rest a bit. It is terribly hot, but the room you will sleep in has a very good fan. Come, I will take you there. *(pause, conspiratorially)* Later, I will show you my computer.

Scene Three

(The next day. Arustu's study. **ARUSTU** *is pouring water over* **RACHEL***'s head.)*

RACHEL. Ah. Relief.

ARUSTU. It is the only way to stay alive in this heat.

RACHEL. You're a wise man.

ARUSTU. They tell me so. I trust you slept well?

RACHEL. Yes, thank you.

ARUSTU. So today you will visit the Taj Mahal?

RACHEL. No, I'll take today to get acclimated. I'll start the hardcore tourist stuff tomorrow.

ARUSTU. So you will visit the sights and write down what you see.

RACHEL. What I see, what I hear, what I think. It's kind of a journal-slash-tourist guide: part history, part armchair travel, part gossip. I can pretty much write what I want, as long as it's fun to read.

ARUSTU. And they pay you to do this?

RACHEL. That's right.

ARUSTU. Amazing. Well. On to business. *(rubs his hands together)* Do you have a question in mind?

RACHEL. You know, I'm not really into this astrology stuff.

ARUSTU. No matter. Your skepticism will not prejudice the stars.

RACHEL. What I mean is –

ARUSTU. There is no harm in asking, right? Unless of course you have no unresolved issues in your life?

RACHEL. Oh, I wouldn't say that.

ARUSTU. Well then…

RACHEL. I'm just not sure…

ARUSTU. You don't even have to say it out loud. Simply focus on it very strongly in your mind.

RACHEL. This should be a…personal question?

ARUSTU. Anything you like! Anything at all. *(pause)* You have it?

RACHEL. I guess so. *(pause)* Wait, no. *(long pause as she tries to figure out the right wording for her question)* Okay, I've got it…Okay. Okay.

ARUSTU. And you were born on September 6, 1968* at two o'clock in the afternoon.

RACHEL. Right.

> *(***ARUSTU*** *enters the information into his computer. After a moment, he turns to* **RACHEL.***)*

ARUSTU. I'm getting a mixed signal. Do you have two different questions?

RACHEL. I did at first, but I made them into one.

ARUSTU. Ah, you see, that is the problem. The question was not completely clear. *(pause)* You'd better tell me what it was.

RACHEL. I thought I didn't have to!

ARUSTU. *(shrugs)* If the question had been clear…

RACHEL. But it's private.

ARUSTU. No problem. You will not offend me. One hears all sorts of things in this line of work.

RACHEL. I'm sure. It's just…

ARUSTU. Yes?

RACHEL. I really don't want to share this with the whole family.

ARUSTU. Please, you insult me! This goes without saying. Between the astrologer and the client is complete confidence!

RACHEL. Well. *(pause)* It concerns a friend of mine. A childhood friend, in America. Her name is…Lisa.

ARUSTU. *Acha.* And when was she born?

RACHEL. Born?

ARUSTU. Yes, her birthday. We were checking your stars, not hers. That may explain the confusion.

**Year should be changed so that she is 37 years old.

RACHEL. Oh, I see. Well, she was born the same day I was, actually. In fact, that's how we met. Our mothers met at the hospital. We've known each other all our lives.

ARUSTU. I see. And what about this…Lisa?

RACHEL. Well…She wants to have a baby. But she's, you know, single. Not married. So at first my question was, should Lisa go through with having her baby alone?

ARUSTU. *(startled)* Alone?

RACHEL. Well, not exactly alone, but with her best girl-friend.

ARUSTU. With her *girlfriend?*

RACHEL. She'd raise it with her girlfriend. She'd *conceive* it alone. Via artificial insemination.

ARUSTU. Artificial – ?!

RACHEL. Oh, forget it.

ARUSTU. *(making an effort to contain himself)* No, please, continue. I am sorry. This question is simply…unfamiliar to me.

RACHEL. Okay, so then I thought, no, that's not the whole question. What I really want to ask is: When – if ever – will Lisa meet a man that she wants to spend her life with? Because if she's going to meet him soon, she can wait to have her baby, but if she's not going to meet him until much later, or if he doesn't even exist, she should go ahead with her plan, because she's, you know, running out of time. Besides which she promised her friend…well. Anyway. So then I decided my question should be, "Will Lisa meet her life partner in the next year, or should she go ahead and have her baby now and hope to meet this guy somewhere down the road?"

ARUSTU. I see. Very complicated question. *(He consults the computer.)* Because you have asked a divided question, the stars have given a divided answer. *Either* she will meet her life partner in the next month, *or* she will have her baby alone and meet him several years later. Or both. Possibly both.

RACHEL. Both?

ARUSTU. Yes. It may be that she will meet the man this month, but it will be some time before she realizes it.

RACHEL. You mean she might meet the man and not even know it?

ARUSTU. *(pleased)* Exactly!

RACHEL. That sucks!

ARUSTU. Pardon?

RACHEL. Now I'm gonna go nuts thinking that the man of my...friend's...dreams is right under her nose and she doesn't even know it!

ARUSTU. *(Pause. Tentatively.)* It is difficult to meet men in America?

RACHEL. Meeting them is easy. Finding someone you want to commit to who wants to commit to you – that's the problem.

ARUSTU. We are fortunate not to have this problem. We are traditional people – our parents tell us whom we should marry and we obey them.

RACHEL. What if it doesn't work out?

ARUSTU. That is not an option. Divorce would humiliate our families. If my wife and I have a problem, my first thought is: "How can I resolve this?" I do not think, "Hmm, perhaps I will take another wife." I know I must continue living with this one, so my only choice is: do I live with her in conflict, or do I make peace in my home?

RACHEL. There's something to be said for that.

ARUSTU. *(delicately)* You yourself are single, are you not?

RACHEL. Me? Yes. As a matter of fact, I am.

ARUSTU. If you like, we can place an advertisement for you. Since fate has brought you to us, you might as well use the time wisely.

RACHEL. An advertisement?

ARUSTU. We can advertise for a sober, educated young man with a good job and a steady disposition. Even at your age, there will be many who will be eager for the chance to live in America. *(He looks at her mischievously.)*

RACHEL. You're joking. Aren't you?

ARUSTU. You had better find someone quickly. You seem to be beautiful now, but who knows how long that will last? We can place the advertisement and see what happens.

RACHEL. Don't you dare.

ARUSTU. *(playful)* Oh, but I will. It just might be the answer to your prayers.

Scene Four

(Four days later. **ANJALI** *and* **RACHEL** *are on the phone.*
ANJALI *is in her bedroom,* **RACHEL** *is in a bedroom at
the Sharma's house.)*

ANJALI. Hello?

RACHEL. It's Rachel.

ANJALI. Rachel! How are you? How is India?

RACHEL. It's great! I've been wanting to call you all week.
How are *you?*

ANJALI. Fine. *(pause)* Actually I'm still sick all the time, but
they tell me that's a good thing.

RACHEL. Poor Anj.

ANJALI. At least the baby's healthy. That's all that matters,
right?

RACHEL. Yeah, knock on wood. *(pause)* So when's the big
ultrasound?

ANJALI. A week from Monday.

RACHEL. Are you gonna find out if it's a boy or girl?

ANJALI. I haven't decided yet.

RACHEL. Please find out.

ANJALI. Why?

RACHEL. I hate suspense.

ANJALI. I'll keep that in mind. *(pause)* Are you enjoying my
family?

RACHEL. They're great.

ANJALI. And my grandmother? She doesn't frighten you?

RACHEL. Haven't met her yet. She's out of town till the end
of the month.

ANJALI. Too bad. I was counting on her to whip you into
shape.

RACHEL. I'm not sure I appreciate that. Which reminds
me, guess what Arustu did.

ANJALI. What?

RACHEL. He put an ad in the paper for a husband for me!

ANJALI. No.

RACHEL. Yes! Now some guy is coming on Saturday to meet me.

ANJALI. Oh my God. He'll probably be expecting a traditional Indian girl.

RACHEL. I know! It's so embarrassing.

ANJALI. Well, try to be on your best behaviour. Who knows? You might get lucky.

RACHEL. Yeah right. And you'd kill me!

ANJALI. You got that right. *(pause)* So have they asked about me?

RACHEL. Of course.

ANJALI. And?

RACHEL. I told them you were busy with your dissertation.

ANJALI. Nothing else?

RACHEL. Nope.

ANJALI. You sure? No accidental slips?

RACHEL. Accidental slips? Like what? "By the way, your cousin the pregnant lesbian – " *Oops! (covers her mouth)*

ANJALI. Shhh… Rachel! Keep your voice down!

RACHEL. My voice *is* down. Anyway, they've got the TV on in there. Now stop worrying. At least about this. Worry about more important things. *(stagey whisper)* And call me as soon as you know if it's got a willy or not.

Scene Five

(Two days later. The Sharmas' living room. **ARUSTU** *is reading a magazine.* **CHANDRA** *is holding* **SACHI**. **OSHO** *is pushing a toy car back and forth across the floor, making engine sounds.* **RACHEL** *paces nervously.)*

CHANDRA. Stop that noise, naughty boy.

*(***OSHO*** is silent for a moment, then starts again.)*

CHANDRA. Ay! Go to the other room.

OSHO. No, Mummy, no, Mummy.

CHANDRA. Then hush.

(A loud noise comes from the kitchen, followed by a little scream. **RACHEL** *jumps, screams as well.)*

CHANDRA. *(explaining)* Sunita is making chai.

RACHEL. Oh, for God's sake. I can't do this!

ARUSTU. You have only to meet him. He is a kind man – I spoke to him on the telephone. *(A knock is heard. Smiling.)* I will answer that.

RACHEL. Oh God.

ARUSTU. Come in! Your good name?

ABHI. Abhi.

ARUSTU. Come in, Abhiji. It is our pleasure. And here is the blushing bride.

RACHEL. *(in extreme embarrassment)* Hi. I'm Rachel Freed.

ABHI. *Namaste.*

RACHEL. *Namaste.*

ARUSTU. Turn around, please, Abhiji.

ABHI. Hm?

ARUSTU. Turn around. Let us look at you.

*(***ABHI*** turns around.* **RACHEL** *looks away, extremely embarrassed.)*

Now why don't you show Miss Freed your arm muscle?

RACHEL. Oh, that won't be necessary.

ARUSTU. No, I insist. This is how it is done here, no problem. Go ahead, Abhiji.

(ABHI *pulls up his sleeve and makes a muscle.*)

Is it okay?

RACHEL. Very nice.

ARUSTU. And perhaps you would like to inspect his teeth?

RACHEL. What?

ARUSTU. His teeth! To see if he has good genetic material.

RACHEL. Look, you guys, this is…

ARUSTU. Show her your teeth, Abhiji.

(ABHI *gives* ARUSTU *a dirty look, then pulls back his lips with his fingers, exposing his teeth.*)

ARUSTU. Well?

RACHEL. *(mortified)* They look fine.

(*At this point* OSHO *can contain himself no longer and starts giggling. Soon everyone in the room except* RACHEL *is howling with laughter.* ARUSTU *and* OSHO *imitate* ABHI *showing off his teeth.*)

ARUSTU. Did you hear her? They look fine! They do not look fine, Abhiji! You should brush them more often!

RACHEL. What the…?

ARUSTU. And that muscle is pathetic! *(pointing at* OSHO*)* His muscle is bigger than that!

(OSHO *makes a muscle.*)

CHANDRA. *(crossing to* RACHEL.*)* Arustu, you are unkind. Look at the poor girl!

RACHEL. *(finally understanding that she's been had)* Arustu, I'm gonna kill you!

(*She chases him around the room. He grabs* OSHO *and uses him as a shield.*)

ARUSTU. You will not harm an innocent child!

RACHEL. No, but I will harm his guilty father! *(She pinches him.)*

ARUSTU. Ow! *(runs to the other side of the couch)* But there is no harm done, eh? And I have found you a very knowledgeable guide, an excellent friend and a cousin of mine, to escort you to see the Taj Mahal.

RACHEL. Cousin! You mean this is –

ARUSTU. My cousin, Abhinav Sharma!

(**ABHI** *smiles sheepishly.*)

RACHEL. *(to* **ARUSTU***)* So you didn't even place the ad?

ARUSTU. No!

RACHEL. What was that you showed me in the paper yesterday – "Suitable groom wanted for intelligent woman living in America?"

ARUSTU. Some family is seeking a husband for their overseas daughter. Now go and enjoy the Taj.

CHANDRA. And here is something to help you stay cool.

(*She and* **ARUSTU** *pick up glasses of water and pour them simultaneously over* **RACHEL***'s and* **ABHI***'s heads. Lights out.*)

Scene Six

(The Taj Mahal. **RACHEL** *and* **ABHI** *stand gazing at the monument.)*

RACHEL. There it is. "The Greatest Monument to Love Ever Created."

ABHI. *(nods uncomfortably)* Yes.

RACHEL. *(pause)* I can't believe Arustu pulled that stunt.

ABHI. *(awkward)* Yes. He is quite –

RACHEL. And you, too!

ABHI. I am sorry. Arustu – that is – it is not my usual –

RACHEL. It's okay, forget it. *(pause, looking again at the Taj)* It's so…*graceful.*

ABHI. *(pleased)* Yes, that is precisely it. It is grateful. I mean, graceful. *(He is immediately shy again. Long awkward pause.)* Shall we approach?

(They begin walking toward the Taj.)

RACHEL. So… I hear you're quite the history buff.

ABHI. Sorry?

RACHEL. That you know a lot about history.

ABHI. *(Shakes his head. Modestly.)* It is only a hobby.

RACHEL. That's not what I hear.

ABHI. My cousins are too kind.

RACHEL. *(pulls out a small pad)* Would you mind if I ask you a few questions about this place, for the piece that I'm writing?

ABHI. About Agra?

RACHEL. About the Taj.

ABHI. *(flattered)* I'm certainly no expert…

RACHEL. I'll be the judge of that.

(Pause. She refers to her notes and takes more during the following questions, which should follow one another rapidly.)

I understand it took more than twenty years to build it?

ABHI. That's right. Twenty-two years.

RACHEL. And this was in the seventeenth century...

ABHI. Construction began in 1630 and was completed in 1652.

RACHEL. And the Taj Mahal is actually a tomb?

ABHI. Correct. Emperor Shah Jahan commissioned it as both a mausoleum for his wife and an enduring tribute to the splendor of their love. Upon his death, he was buried alongside her in the vault beneath the main chamber.

RACHEL. How many people?

ABHI. Sorry?

RACHEL. I understand there was a huge body of labor –

ABHI. Oh. Yes. More than 20,000 workers.

RACHEL. *(shaking her head)* Incredible.

ABHI. *(Warming to the subject. Lecturing.)* A thousand elephants carried the materials from all over Asia. When it was finished, the emperor Shah Jahan cut off the right hand of the master builder so that it could never be repeated.

RACHEL. That puts a bit of a damper on the monument to love.

ABHI. Pardon?

RACHEL. Chopping off the guy's hand. Not very romantic.

ABHI. Well, it –

RACHEL. *(making a note as she talks)* What's so romantic about building a monument when the money comes from other people's taxes and you don't have to carry a single stone? Now if the king had cut off his *own* hand, that would be another story.

ABHI. *(stiffly)* Emperor.

RACHEL. Hmmm?

ABHI. Shah Jahan was an emperor. Not a king.

RACHEL. Same difference, no?

ABHI. An emperor rules over an entire empire. A king generally governs only a single nation.

RACHEL. I stand corrected.

ABHI. *(annoyed)* Shah Jahan may have been a tyrant – they all were in those days – but there is no doubt that he genuinely adored his wife. *(pause)* His second wife, that is.

RACHEL. *Second* wife?

ABHI. *(sheepish)* Even the royalty could not always do as they chose.

(RACHEL is about to ask him another question, but he gestures that they should go in.)

Come. We must remove our shoes to enter.

(They remove their shoes and enter the building. A sign reads "It is an offense to make the monument dirty." A couple of other people enter in the shadows and mill around, looking at the walls.)

RACHEL. *(examining the marble)* It's so intricate.

ABHI. *(professorial)* Shah Jahan planned to build a second one, out of black marble, on the other side of the river, but he died before the foundation was complete.

RACHEL. It's like he cherished his suffering.

ABHI. Precisely. He immortalized it. The Taj Mahal is "a solitary teardrop hanging on the cheek of time."

RACHEL. *(raising her eyebrows)* So you're a poet.

ABHI. Not me. Rabindranath Tagore.

RACHEL. Ah. *(makes a note)* You don't write poetry?

ABHI. No.

RACHEL. Never?

ABHI. *(conceding)* Occasionally. But only my God can bear to hear it. And that is because he tunes his ears to the intention rather than the result.

RACHEL. Oh, I'm sure that's not –

ABHI. Come. *(quickly changing the subject)* Each of these flowers contains more than fifty separate pieces of stone.

RACHEL. *(Smiles. Makes a note.)* Do they sell any diagrams that list the different gems?

ABHI. Not that I know of. *(pause)* But I can identify them
for you, if you'd like.

RACHEL. You can? *(ABHI nods.)* Please.

ABHI. *(Pointing. Moving slowly from place to place. Lighting
shifts and becomes magical. Music or drone fades in. These
effects, together with the lyrical names of the stones, cast a
hypnotic spell.)*

Carnelian. Turquoise. Lapis Lazuli. Coral. Onyx. Cat's
eye. Garnet. Jasper. Ruby. Jade. Goldstone. Agate.
Slate. Diamond. Malachite. Sapphire. Topaz. Ame-
thyst. Emerald. Conch shell. Sandstone. Bloodstone.
Mother of Pearl.

RACHEL. *(pause)* It's spooky.

ABHI. What?

RACHEL. The echo in here. It's as if a ghost were repeating
your words.

ABHI. Yes. That is one of the things I like about this place.
It feels as if they are all still in here – Shah Jahan,
Mumtaz Mahal, the courtiers, even the builders –
lurking in the shadows, waiting to tell their stories to
anyone who will listen.

RACHEL. Mmmm. *(smiles)* So you said the woman Shah
Jahan built this for was not his first wife?

ABHI. That is correct. *(Pause. Explaining)* A prince's marriage was a political arrangement. And he was so
young when he first saw her.

RACHEL. Saw who?

ABHI. Arjumand Banu Begam was her name. Later she was
known as Mumtaz Mahal, "the Chosen of the Palace."

*(Pause. RACHEL takes out her pad and begins to make
some notes.)*

Shah Jahan – who was still Prince Khurram at the time
– was only sixteen years old when he spotted her hawk-
ing glass beads at the Royal Meena Bazaar.

*(Lights shift and a woman steps out of the shadows,
dressed in period costume. Music comes up slowly, either*

classical Indian music or some kind of Bollywood East/
West mix. The movement and acting in this section
should be stylized and theatrical.)

RACHEL. Wait a minute.

*(***ARJUMAND*** stops and looks at* ***RACHEL****)*

The empress-to-be was a salesgirl?

*(***ARJUMAND*** tosses her head scornfully.)*

ABHI. Not quite.

*(***ARJUMAND*** smiles and continues her cross.)*

On an ordinary day, Arjumand Banu Begam was a high-born girl, the daughter of a prime minister. But on an ordinary day the prince would not have been permitted to enter the bazaar at all. It was at the Royal Meena Bazaar that the ladies of the court purchased the oils, waxes and dyes that were the hidden complements to their beauty. Men were strictly forbidden to enter. But a couple of times a year, they had what they called "upside-down days," in which the shop girls stayed home, the ladies became the merchants, and the male courtiers became the customers. On such days all decorum was abandoned, and the ladies and courtiers haggled as if it were an ordinary marketplace. The courtiers even attempted to impress the maidens by haggling with them in rhyming poetry.

RACHEL. Such as?

ABHI. Pardon?

RACHEL. The poetry. What was it like?

ABHI. Oh, I don't know exactly. "Oh lady fair, your face is rare," something like that.

RACHEL. Go on.

ABHI. Excuse me?

RACHEL. What else would they say?

ABHI. I don't know…They'd try to flatter the women and get a good price for themselves at the same time. Perhaps something like…

*(A second **LADY** steps out of the shadows. **ABHI** takes on the role of the courtier, stepping into the scene and addressing her. He should be substantially transformed while playing the role.)*

ABHI. *(cont.)* How much do you ask for this bangle here?

LADY. Twenty rupees – it's not so dear.

ABHI. Twenty rupees! Don't be unkind!
  'Tis true your beauty makes men blind,
  But velvet skin and sparkling eyes
  And shining hair cannot disguise,
  This trifle's not as fine as you –
  I'll pay five rupees…but give me two.

LADY. *(indignant)* Five rupees! Ha!
  This bangle's wrought of gold and jewels,
  Beyond the ken of silly fools,
  It's lovely as the road is long.
  You'll pay ten rupees – and a song!

ABHI. To sing for you, my voice would quake
  my hands would shake, your ears would ache
  I'll give eight rupees and a kiss
  To transport you to endless bliss.

*(He goes to kiss the **LADY** on the lips. She playfully turns her head at the last minute so that he kisses her cheek.)*

RACHEL. Bravo! *(excited)* Was it really like that?

ABHI. *(revved up)* Of course! *(pause)* Except that they were speaking in Persian.

*(**RACHEL** is about to ask another question, but he stops her. He is finding his form.)*

Now shhh. No more questions. It is bad luck to interrupt the storyteller.

It was on an upside-down day in 1607 that Prince Khurram walked into the bazaar and saw a young girl selling pieces of glass cut to look like precious gems.

*(A **YOUNG MAN** emerges, dressed as Prince Khurram. **ABHI** shadows him throughout this narration.)*

ABHI. *(cont.)* There was no one at her stand, because the girl's beauty was so flawless, so radiant, that the young men were too intimidated to approach. The prince strode up to her booth and asked the price of the largest gem, an enormous piece of glass the size of a pomegranate, which glittered in the sun like a diamond.

(to **ARJUMAND***)* How much for this one?

She gave him a saucy look and told him the jewel was so expensive…

ARJUMAND. *(overlapping)* This jewel is so expensive that even the emperor himself cannot afford it.

ABHI. When he insisted she tell him the price, she said the cost was…

ARJUMAND. Ten thousand rupees.

ABHI. He looked at her for a full minute, until even in the role of a cheeky shop girl, she was compelled to drop her eyes. He then removed his purse, took out ten thousand rupees, handed them to her, and departed without a word.

(The following narration is played out in a kind of stylized gesture/dance.)

The next afternoon, the prince did something very unusual. He asked his father's permission to marry the young woman he had met at the Royal Meena Bazaar. His father smiled a mysterious smile, remembering the moment he first set eyes on Nur Jahan, his own beloved queen. The emperor granted his son's wish, but not right away. First the prince was married off to a Persian princess to forge an alliance. Five years later he was permitted to marry his true love.

RACHEL. Not such a great deal for the Persian princess.

(Lights out on historical characters.)

ABHI. *(shrugs)* Who knows? *(smiling)* She may have been relieved to get away from him. The prince was fond of attending executions in the torture chambers below the palace. Death by strangulation was his favorite spectator sport.

(Strangulation sounds are heard. The assembled crowd gives a cheer.)

RACHEL. Now *that's* romantic.

ABHI. In any case, the prince adored his new bride. From their wedding day onward, the two were never apart. When Mumtaz Mahal died while giving birth to their fourteenth child, Shah Jahan was devastated. He locked himself in his rooms, and for eight days he took no food or drink. When he came out, his black hair had turned completely white. Some even say he had shrunk from a tall man to a short one. He ordered his whole kingdom into mourning, and for two years no games or music or bright colors were permitted in public places. He himself wore nothing but white robes for ten full years in honor of the queen's death.

(Pause. Lights out on characters.)

Whatever else you might say about the man, you cannot accuse him of inconstancy in love.

RACHEL. *(impressed and becoming more curious about him)* You're not by any chance a professional guide?

ABHI. *(embarrassed)* No, just a student of history. And a teacher.

RACHEL. What do you teach?

ABHI. I teach Hindi. To foreigners. And sometimes to cabinet ministers from South India. *(pause)* Shall we descend to the vault?

Scene Seven

(That evening. The Sharmas' living room. RACHEL sits on the couch, holding SACHI. ARUSTU is reading the newspaper. CHANDRA is quizzing OSHO on English spelling words. OSHO writes them in his book as he speaks the letters.)

CHANDRA. Drill.

OSHO. D-R-I-L-L.

CHANDRA. Bore.

OSHO. B-O-R-E.

ARUSTU. So…How did you enjoy our cousin Abhiji?

RACHEL. He's an interesting guy. Quite a fount of information, once you get him going.

CHANDRA. Spigot.

OSHO. S-P-I-G-O-T.

ARUSTU. Shall I check your charts for compatibility?

RACHEL. What? Oh. No, thanks.

ARUSTU. Abhi's chart predicts many offspring. All the men in our family are very fertile.

CHANDRA. Finger.

(OSHO continues writing the words without speaking them aloud.)

RACHEL. Thanks, but no thanks. *(pause)* I do envy you, though.

ARUSTU. Me?

RACHEL. Having all this family around. My life seems so isolated by comparison.

CHANDRA. Zoo.

ARUSTU. *(with a small sigh)* We are never lonely here.

RACHEL. Isn't that a good thing?

CHANDRA. Axe. *(Her pronunciation is somewhere between "axe," "ex," and "eggs.")*

OSHO. *Kya?*

ARUSTU. *(shrugs)* There is no changing it, so what is the point of asking oneself that question?

CHANDRA. Axe!

(**OSHO** *writes.* **CHANDRA** *picks up his paper to see what he has written.*)

ARUSTU. But I will tell you one thing. *(leaning in)* You can have no secrets in this house.

CHANDRA. *(to* **OSHO***)* How do you spell axe?

OSHO. *(fearfully)* E-G-G-S.

ARUSTU. E-G-G-S is the correct spelling of "eggs." *(to* **RACHEL***)* Would you pronounce axe "eggs?" *(to* **OSHO***)* Axe.

OSHO. *(catching on)* A-X-E!

ARUSTU. *Acha! (to* **RACHEL***)* If his mother had correct pronunciation...

CHANDRA. *(shooting* **ARUSTU** *a dirty look)* Finger!

OSHO. F-I-N-G-E-R.

CHANDRA. *(to* **RACHEL***)* Is he spelling this word correctly?

RACHEL. Yes.

CHANDRA. And look at what is written here. *(holds out workbook)* F-A-I-G-E-R. You see! He knows it, but he does it wrong! This proves he is not serious about his studies. *(to* **OSHO***)* Button.

OSHO. B-U-T-T-N-E.

CHANDRA. *(menacing)* N-E?

OSHO. *(panicked)* B-U-T-T-E-N!

CHANDRA. But-*ten?*

OSHO. I-N?

CHANDRA. I-N?

OSHO. *(whimpering)* E-N?

CHANDRA. O-N! B-U-T-T-O-N!

OSHO. But-tone?

CHANDRA. *Hey Bhagwan!* Not but-tone, button. *(to* **ARUSTU***)* Will it disturb you now if I beat him?

ARUSTU. Yes, it will disturb me very much.

CHANDRA. He has made seven mistakes.

ARUSTU. So what?

CHANDRA. He is habituated to be beaten.

ARUSTU. But I am not habituated to watch it.

CHANDRA. Then you go in the other room. I will beat him.

ARUSTU. He will become repulsive to his studies. *(He exits.)*

CHANDRA. *Eh!* (*Making a "good riddance" gesture. To* **RACHEL**) At his age, I was an excellent student. First in the class. Look at this, from his school. Here he has made the same mistakes twice. This shows that he is not serious. And look here – he has missed one, and not completed two of the questions. And here. It says capitalize every word. He has capitalized all except one. *Why?* Do you think this is his best work?

RACHEL. I don't know. I suppose he could do better.

CHANDRA. He *can* do better! (*notices that* **RACHEL** *is staring at her*) Why do you look at me like that? He does not mind if I beat him. It is good for him. He loves me, don't you Osho?

OSHO. Yes.

ARUSTU. *(from offstage)* He answers out of fear.

CHANDRA. He does not. Do you, Osho?

OSHO. No.

CHANDRA. Now come here and give your mother a kiss.

(**OSHO** *hugs and kisses her.* **CHANDRA** *nods toward* **RACHEL**.)

OSHO. *(dutifully, to* **RACHEL**) I love my mummy.

CHANDRA. You see? Now go and continue working, naughty boy. You have escaped a beating this time.

(**OSHO** *exits.*)

You see how Arustu insults me? But he never involves himself with the boy's studies, oh no! The boy could spend all day roaming the streets like a hooligan and he would not even notice.

ARUSTU. *(from offstage)* Falsely accused! I am falsely accused!

(**SACHI** *starts to cry and* **CHANDRA** *takes her from* **RACHEL**.)

CHANDRA. Sunita!

(**SUNITA** *enters, takes* **SACHI** *from* **CHANDRA** *and exits.*)

RACHEL. *(looking after* **SUNITA***)* She looks so young.

CHANDRA. Who?

RACHEL. Sunita.

CHANDRA. She is seventeen.

RACHEL. Does she go to school?

CHANDRA. No. Her parents are very poor. She is lucky to have such a comfortable job. Her parents could just as easily have cut off her fingers and sent her out on the streets to beg.

RACHEL. What?

CHANDRA. You have seen the beggar children, haven't you? With the missing fingers?

RACHEL. I thought it was leprosy.

CHANDRA. Sometimes. Sometimes not.

RACHEL. Parents cut off their own...

CHANDRA. If they are desperate enough. The streets are competitive. People have more sympathy for beggars who are missing some body parts. But even among those who are better off, many families still do not believe in educating girls.

RACHEL. I take it your parents were more liberal.

CHANDRA. I was lucky to be born into an enlightened class. *(with some pride)* I completed my PhD in Chemistry the year before Osho was born.

RACHEL. Really!

CHANDRA. I was nominated for a faculty appointment.

RACHEL. But you didn't –

CHANDRA. I had to withdraw my name. Mrs. Sharma will not permit me to work.

RACHEL. I thought she was a school principal.

CHANDRA. *(nodding)* She has one thousand pupils in her charge. She raised five children, born over a twenty-year span, working all the while. Even now, she travels the country, giving lectures. She sits on so many boards and committees.

RACHEL. So why...?

CHANDRA. It is different, I suppose, what you do for yourself and what you want for your son. Perhaps she feels she was not a good wife to her own husband. He is a politician, also traveling all the time. The two of them hardly meet. *(pause)* I don't mean to speak badly of her. I admire her very much. *(lowering her voice)* It is only that when she is here, we cannot relax. She demands old-fashioned respect. Even Arustu is afraid of her. When she is home, I must keep my head covered at all times. And she does not permit me to see friends.

RACHEL. Why?

CHANDRA. What does a woman need friends for if she is married? That is how the thinking goes. Our husbands and children should be our whole lives. Even my family I should see only once or twice a year.

(SUNITA enters with SACHI, hands her to CHANDRA, exits.)

Everything is changing, though. My path is settled, but it will be different for her. *(indicating SACHI)* I want her to go to Oxford. Or maybe Cambridge.

RACHEL. But you won't beat her, will you?

CHANDRA. No... She is too small. *(pause)* But if she is lazy in her studies, I will beat her. How can she have a better life if she will not study? *(Looking at SACHI. Tenderly, in baby talk)* If I have to beat you, I will do so, never fear.

Scene Eight

(Three days later. ANJALI *and* RACHEL, *on the phone. As before,* ANJALI *is in her bedroom, and* RACHEL *is in a bedroom at the Sharma's house.)*

ANJALI. *(excited)* It's a girl.

RACHEL. *(screams)* Oh my *God!*

ARUSTU. *(from offstage)* Rachel? Are you alright?

RACHEL. *(to* ARUSTU*)* Fine! *(softer, to* ANJALI*)* I'm so excited!

ANJALI. Me too! She seems so much more *real* now. I had to pull over and cry on the way home from the hospital. I just kept thinking, "I'm having a little girl." *(Her eyes fill.)*

RACHEL. Oh sweetie.

ANJALI. And then suddenly I was terrified. I thought, how can I protect her?

RACHEL. From what?

ANJALI. You know…All the crap. All those societal voices that tell her she has to look a certain way and act a certain way and *be* a certain way. Everything that made me feel so inadequate growing up.

RACHEL. Ah, but she'll have something you didn't.

ANJALI. What?

RACHEL. She'll have you as a role model.

ANJALI. Oh, come on, me? What kind of role model am I? I'm a coward. I'm not even out to my own family.

RACHEL. You are a courageous warrior goddess, is what you are.

ANJALI. Please.

RACHEL. You tell the truth, and you follow through. You say you'll do something, and there it is: done. These are extremely rare qualities.

ANJALI. Well thank you.

RACHEL. Plus, she's growing up in San Francisco.

ANJALI. Yes, thank God for that. There are bound to be kids in her class whose parents are more peculiar than we are.

RACHEL. Oooh yeah. Big-time.

ANJALI. Rachel....

RACHEL. Yeah?

ANJALI. Does it ever strike you as selfish, what we're doing?

RACHEL. What do you mean?

ANJALI. Bringing children into the world just because we *want* to?

RACHEL. What other reason is there? Should we do it because someone else wants us to?

ANJALI. But on our incomes, with so little outside support? I think of my family in India, whenever a baby is born. So many aunties and uncles around; so many pairs of arms just waiting to help.

RACHEL. You can have that in San Francisco, too. There's community out there. We'll just have to work a little harder to find it, that's all.

ANJALI. I guess.

RACHEL. You'll be a great mom.

ANJALI. I hope so.

RACHEL. Anyway, it's a little late in the game to start second-guessing yourself.

ANJALI. I know.

RACHEL. So cut it out.

ANJALI. I'll try. *(pause)* Anyway, I should go –

RACHEL. Uh uh! Not without telling me.

ANJALI. What?

RACHEL. Her name!

ANJALI. Whose?

RACHEL. Whose.

ANJALI. How do you know I've picked it?

RACHEL. Haven't you?

ANJALI. Yes.

RACHEL. See?

ANJALI. But I wasn't going to tell anyone yet.

RACHEL. Come on. You can tell Auntie Rachel.

ANJALI. Oh all right, but it's a secret, okay?

RACHEL. Cross my heart.

ANJALI. Meera. Meera Janaki Sharma Narayan. After my mother.

Scene Nine

(The Baby Taj. Music. The following text is enacted in a stylized dance/pantomime.)

ABHI. They say the birth of Nur Jahan, in 1577, was surrounded by miracles.

Nur Jahan's father was a Persian nobleman who had fallen on hard times. Pursued by political enemies, he and his pregnant wife fled their native country on foot. In the desert, the woman gave birth to a baby girl. Since they had little food or water, the couple left the child in the desert, hoping someone more fortunate would take pity on her.

As they departed, a king cobra approached the infant. The snake took one look at the tiny exquisite face and, instead of striking the baby dead, appointed itself her champion. With the great cobra's protection, the child survived the pitiless assault of the noonday sun. This was the first miracle.

It wasn't long before scouts from a passing caravan discovered the hungry infant. They went in search of a wet nurse for the baby, and soon caught up with the child's own parents! This was the next miracle.

They delivered the family to the Royal Court, where the father rose to a position of power. The baby grew into a young woman of such spectacular beauty that passers-by had to shield their eyes from the radiance of her countenance. She was an expert archer, and a magnificent poet and painter. Most miraculous of all, she captured the hardened heart of the Emperor Jahangir. After their marriage, she became a partner in governing, whose wisdom in affairs of state is now as legendary as her beauty.

*(Lights up on **RACHEL** and **ABHI**, who sit in the grass, eating lunch. **RACHEL** jots notes on a pad.)*

RACHEL. So let me get this straight. We're talking about Nur Jahan – Emperor Jahangir's wife and Prince Khurram's mother. *(noting down relationships)*

ABHI. Right.

RACHEL. And her phenomenal talents included archery, painting, poetry, and politics.

ABHI. Correct.

RACHEL. And on top of all that, she was such a dutiful, loving daughter that she built this tomb – the Baby Taj – for her father when he died, even though in childhood he almost left her in the desert to perish.

ABHI. Yes.

RACHEL. Don't you think that's a bit much?

ABHI. These are ancient legends, Miss Freed. The royalty lock their enemies in towers, they slay their own brothers, they throw themselves in the river in the name of love. They live more boldly than we ever could. That is why they compel our attention.

RACHEL. Okay, I accept that, but why is it the women are always saints? The men run around murdering people and wreaking havoc, but the women are always the pictures of virtue and nothing short of Miss World in the looks department.

ABHI. I cannot say. The stories are not of my invention.

RACHEL. I'll tell you why. Because it's men passing the stories down. And they aren't interested in the reality of women. *(pause)* How did you learn all these stories, anyway?

ABHI. My father used to tell them to me –

RACHEL. Well there you go. Is he a teacher too?

ABHI. He was. A far better one than I. He taught Hindi to the prime minister.

RACHEL. He's retired?

ABHI. He died fourteen years ago, on my twenty-first birthday.

RACHEL. I'm sorry.

ABHI. He was ill for many years. He was determined to remain alive until I reached manhood. *(Pause. Wryly)* He was a patient man. And a precise one. Words, the right words, were his whole life. *(Pause. Tentatively)* Miss Freed...

RACHEL. Rachel. Please. We've known each other a week and a half; we've spent almost three entire days together. I think you can call me by my first name.

ABHI. *(awkward)* Alright. Rachel. *(pause)* If it is not too impolite a question...

RACHEL. Yes?

ABHI. How did you become so...

RACHEL. What?

ABHI. I don't know. The things you say. They seem so... *(searches for a word)*

RACHEL. What?

ABHI. Bitter, perhaps?

RACHEL. *Bitter?* I'm *bitter?*

ABHI. No, bitter is not right, but...cynical, maybe? Disenchanted?

RACHEL. Wow, you're a regular thesaurus.

ABHI. I am sorry. I –

RACHEL. But enough with the compliments. Tell me what you really think.

ABHI. I did not mean to –

RACHEL. Hey, I can take it. I get called bitter, cynical and disenchanted every day. I have a T-shirt, in fact, "BCDWG" – Bitter, cynical, disenchanted white girl.

ABHI. Perhaps we should –

RACHEL. What? Now you wanna go home? Can't take another moment of my bitter, cynical, disenchanted presence?

ABHI. Please, Miss Freed.

RACHEL. Rachel!

ABHI. Rachel. Please. I did not mean...Forget I said anything. More chapattis?

(She takes one and they sit in silence for a moment.)

RACHEL. I guess I am a bit...disenchanted, if you want to put it that way. I have reason to be. Especially about all that romantic crap. I've been there and back, you know?

ABHI. *(his curiosity giving him courage)* You have been married?

RACHEL. *(surprised)* Married? No. I've just had a lot of stupid relationships. That's the way we do things in my country. Trial and error.

ABHI. You were unhappy in these...relationships?

RACHEL. Unhappy? Sometimes. Sometimes I was wildly happy, for about ten minutes. Until the veil dropped, and my handsome prince and I saw each other for the needy, neurotic humans we really were and ran screaming in opposite directions. *(pause)* How about you? How's your love life going?

ABHI. Me? *(laughs)* Our visit to the Taj Mahal was the first time I'd been alone with a woman who was not my mother in more than three years.

RACHEL. You're kidding.

ABHI. Not at all.

RACHEL. Why?

ABHI. In India, we do not date. Not so much. Some do, the younger people, in Delhi. But outside of the city we are more traditional. We are introduced, and then we marry.

RACHEL. So why aren't you married? Aren't you a little old to be single?

ABHI. If I were not so well brought up, I might ask you the same question.

RACHEL. *(smiles)* I'd feel let down if you didn't.

ABHI. I should have been married this past year.

RACHEL. What happened?

ABHI. It did not work out.

RACHEL. Was it an arranged marriage?

ABHI. Yes.

RACHEL. That whole concept is so amazing to me. Didn't you want to, you know, fall in love? Like Shah Jahan?

ABHI. I tried for years to find my love match, but I could not find her.

RACHEL. So you gave up?

ABHI. I was thirty-five years old. I wanted to get on with my life.

RACHEL. What did you do?

ABHI. What everyone does. I asked my mother and uncle to arrange a marriage for me.

RACHEL. I bet they were stoked.

ABHI. Stoke –

RACHEL. Thrilled.

ABHI. Oh yes. They were so "stoked." They placed an ad in the newspaper the next day; they were terrified I would change my mind. They conducted several interviews, and out of those they selected a suitable girl.

*(A **GIRL** appears on the side of the stage.)*

Her family was not wealthy, but they were Brahmins, like ourselves, and the girl was educated, pursuing an advanced degree at the university. My mother organized an engagement party, and the girl and I were introduced.

RACHEL. How was it?

ABHI. We were both terribly nervous. We could hardly speak to one another. Finally I said, *(to the **GIRL**)* "You seem very nice, but you should go on a diet."

RACHEL. *(screams in disbelief)* I can't believe you said that! Is that why the marriage didn't go through?

ABHI. *(surprised)* Not at all. She said,

GIRL. So should you too.

*(**ABHI** and the **GIRL** both laugh.)*

RACHEL. Oh my God. If you told an American woman to go on a diet, she'd sock you in the mouth.

ABHI. But why should she, when it was clear that I should do the same thing myself?

RACHEL. American women are very sensitive about such matters.

ABHI. This girl was not so sensitive.

(*The* **GIRL** *giggles and disappears.*)

RACHEL. So what happened?

ABHI. The wedding date was set. It is customary for the bride's family to pay for the wedding, but as the girl's parents were not well off, my mother was concerned about what kind of ceremony they could afford. My father was very well connected, so there would be many dignitaries and officials at the wedding. She felt that the reception should meet certain standards.

(**MOTHER** *appears onstage.*)

MOTHER. (*in a tizzy*) What if the prime minister himself should decide to attend? We cannot shame your father's memory.

ABHI. My mother decided to send a message, through a third party.

(*A rather bumbling* **MAN** *enters.*)

MOTHER. You are a close relation of Mrs. Joshi, are you not?

MAN. Madam, she is my mother's first cousin.

MOTHER. If you could be so good as to question her, in a delicate way of course, as to what sort of menu and entertainment she is planning for my son's wedding, I would be very appreciative. Please give her to know that if she should require any assistance whatsoever, our family would be happy to provide it. I rely entirely on your taste and discretion in the handling of this matter.

MAN. I am delighted to be of service.

ABHI. The next day the girl's mother sent a message that the wedding was cancelled. My mother was beside herself.

MOTHER. What exactly did you say to her?

MAN. Only what you asked, Madam.

MOTHER. But you must have done something to offend her!

MAN. Not at all! I simply told her that she should be grateful for your generosity, since everyone knows her husband's gambling is driving her family into bankruptcy.

MOTHER. *Aieeee!*

ABHI. My mother made overtures to the woman, to try and explain, but she refused to listen. Friends tell me that the girl herself was quite upset.

RACHEL. And you?

ABHI. That is the strangest part. I was devastated. More than I would have thought possible. You might think, "I met this girl only once – it is not possible that I could love her." And in fact I would not say that I loved her. But without realizing it, I had gotten used to the idea of this girl. Maybe my image was false, but she seemed to me a quiet, kind, intelligent girl. I was relieved that the searching was over, and eager to bind my life to hers. *(pause)* Can you understand at all?

RACHEL. *(nodding)* I've imagined that sense of relief myself. I've even wished someone would arrange a match for me, so I could get it over with and focus on other things.

ABHI. I believe Arustu is willing to be your matchmaker.

RACHEL. I'm sure he is. But it wouldn't work.

ABHI. How do you know? Perhaps if you approached things in a more logical fashion…

RACHEL. Believe me, I've tried everything. I even tried to arrange my own marriage once.

ABHI. Really?

RACHEL. Uh huh. I had this friend I'd known since elementary school, a guy named Nathan.

*(**NATHAN** appears.)*

RACHEL. *(cont.)* Sweetest guy you ever met. Total salt of the earth. Honest, caring, smart, you name it. Handsome, too! And for years, Nathan and I had complained to each about how we wanted to settle down, we wanted to have kids, everybody out there was a schmuck and a commitmentphobe and yadda yadda yadda.

(crosses to **NATHAN***)*

So one day Nathan was over at my house, and we were moaning about our love lives, as usual, and I said to him, "Why don't we just marry each other?"

NATHAN. Are you serious?

RACHEL. The thought did occur to me.

NATHAN. *(interested)* Really?

RACHEL. I know it sounds weird, but…we both want the same things, and we already love each other. I mean, I *love* you. And I know you love me. And true, it's not "that" kind of love, but I thought, Well, that's because we've known each other so long that we've gotten used to interacting in a certain way, and maybe if we turned the dial just the teeniest bit and looked at each other in a different light, we could… I don't know.

NATHAN. You do know.

*(***NATHAN*** *looks at her for a long moment, then leans in to kiss her. Lights cross-fade.)*

ABHI. So what happened?

RACHEL. I couldn't go through with it. I mean, it was absurd. Ludicrous! We're lying there in bed together and I just… *(to* **NATHAN***)* It's not right.

NATHAN. What?

RACHEL. It feels too strange. It's like I'm in bed with my brother.

NATHAN. I thought this is what you wanted!

RACHEL. I thought so, too. But doesn't it feel awkward?

NATHAN. We knew it would take some getting used to.

RACHEL. *(with finality)* I'm sorry.

NATHAN. You can't just...experiment on people, Rachel! This isn't a game!

RACHEL. I know, I didn't mean to –

NATHAN. Well you should've thought. What was this, just an ego trip for you?

RACHEL. No, I –

NATHAN. I feel like a goddamn idiot!

RACHEL. Oh God, I didn't – I'm sorry, I'm so sorry...

(cross-fade)

ABHI. Are you still friends?

RACHEL. We are. He forgave me, thank God. But it took a while.

ABHI. Why didn't you give the relationship some time to develop?

RACHEL. I wanted to, you have to believe me, but I just... couldn't. There were other times, too, when I was dating someone who was perfectly nice, good-looking, whatever, and I'd kick myself, I'd say, "Give it a chance, dammit," and I'd try, but there always was this voice in my head screaming, *this is not right,* and I had to get out.

And then when I finally did meet someone I wanted to commit to, he was the one with cold feet. The last guy I dated, Sam – we were together on and off for more than two years, and he never made even the most basic kind of commitment. I could barely get him to admit we were in a relationship at all.

SAM. Of course we're in a relationship. We're relating! We see each other almost every day.

RACHEL. *(crossing to* **SAM***)* You know what I mean.

SAM. Whoa, Rachel, we've been over this! What does it change? You were in a "committed" relationship with Jay. He told you exactly what you wanted to hear, and then he cheated on you. You were in a "committed" relationship with Robert before that, and you dumped him! It's hypocrisy!

RACHEL. That's very logical, Sam, but...

SAM. Rachel, this moment is all there is. And as each new moment arises we can choose to be together or not. I could say "I plan to stay with you forever, baby," but all that would mean is that in this moment that's the way it appears to me.

RACHEL. But you can state an *intention*. At the very least we can say that at *this moment,* we're not seeing other people.

SAM. Words.

RACHEL. Sam –

SAM. Words, Rachel! Those are words! Am I seeing anyone else? Am I?

RACHEL. I don't think so.

SAM. You're right! I'm not! Are you?

RACHEL. No.

SAM. Well then. We're not seeing other people.

RACHEL. But – oh, forget it. Forget it. *(to* ABHI*)* And I got so sick of the game, so sick of myself *in* the game... So finally I thought, I've just gotta take myself out of this. We all have different destinies, different paths, and maybe a partnership with a man, in this life, is not my path.

ABHI. But not to have a family, to be alone in the world...

RACHEL. Oh, I still want a family.

ABHI. But I thought you said –

RACHEL. I just can't do the man-woman romance thing, that's all. There are other ways.

ABHI. I don't understand.

RACHEL. I made a plan with my best friend. A woman. Her name is...

(ANJALI *rushes on with a panicked look, afraid* RACHEL*'s about to reveal her identity.)*

Lisa! She's blonde!

ANJALI. Please.

RACHEL. She's a lesbian, I'm straight – but we're sort of... *(looks at* ANJALI*)* soulmates.

*(*ANJALI *smiles.)*

We have this almost telepathic communication. She sees right through me, and she isn't afraid to tell me what she thinks. Which can be hell sometimes, but... It's important to have that, you know? Especially since we're both outsiders in our own families. We're different in many ways, but we do share one key thing.

*(*RACHEL *walks to* ANJALI *and takes one of the glasses.)*

ANJALI. To us.

RACHEL. To us.

ANJALI. The few, the proud.

RACHEL. The many, the shamefaced.

ANJALI. Who suck...

RACHEL. miserably, abominably suck...

RACHEL & ANJALI. ...at romantic relationships.

(They clink glasses, drink.)

RACHEL. *(crossing back to* ABHI*)* We concluded that it made a lot more sense to build a family around friendship, which lasts, rather than around romance, which doesn't. We decided we'd each conceive a child through artificial insemination and raise the children together, as siblings. Then lovers could come and go, but we'd have this stable family to come home to at the end of the day.

ANJALI. *(Doorbell rings.)* There she is. *(She exits.)*

RACHEL. *(to* ABHI*)* This must sound incredibly strange to you.

ABHI. It is outside of my experience. Completely outside. *(Another pause as he digests this. Then he bursts out.)* But what if the child is a boy? A boy needs a father!

RACHEL. *(defensive)* A lot of kids grow up without fathers! Women have been raising children alone since the beginning of time.

ABHI. So you will carry out this plan?

RACHEL. Yes.

ABHI. You have no doubts?

RACHEL. *(hesitant)* No.

ABHI. Then why are you here?

RACHEL. What do you mean?

ABHI. Why are you not with child?

RACHEL. I got this job, so I had to postpone it for a month. As soon as I get back I'm going to start trying.

ABHI. *(unconvinced)* I see.

RACHEL. You don't believe me?

ABHI. I am only wondering.

RACHEL. What?

ABHI. Whether this job might lead to another like it, and then another. Since there was never a right man, perhaps there will also never be a right time.

RACHEL. *(stung)* That…You…Who the hell – You don't even know me!

ABHI. You are right. I don't.

RACHEL. Have you been talking to Anjali or something?

ABHI. *(surprised)* Anjali? I have not spoken to her in years. What does Anjali have to do –

RACHEL. Nothing! I just…I… *(getting control of herself)* Nothing.

ABHI. *(Begins gathering the lunch things. Nervously)* If you have finished eating, perhaps we can view the back of the monument now.

RACHEL. You're not as shy as you pretend to be, are you?

ABHI. I thought I was. Our conversation seems to have emboldened me.

RACHEL. I tend to have that effect on people. Although in this case I'm not so sure it's a good thing, if it means you're going to be busting my chops all the time.

ABHI. Busting your –

RACHEL. Giving me a hard time.

ABHI. I thought you liked that.

RACHEL. What makes you say that?

ABHI. Didn't you prefer the man who gave you the most difficulty?

RACHEL. *(stung again)* That... *(quickly gaining control)* Okay, Doctor Freud, are you analyzing me or flirting with me?

ABHI. *(taken aback)* I –

RACHEL. Or both? Which, I might add, is a very dangerous combination.

ABHI. Neither. Really. I was just making conversation.

RACHEL. Well can we stick with the historical stuff from here on out? I've had about all the soul-searching I can take for one afternoon.

ABHI. Certainly. *(Finishes gathering up the lunch thing. Avoiding her eyes.)* The grounds will close soon anyway. Shall we explore the other side?

RACHEL. Lead on. *(He starts to exit. She watches him for a moment, then follows.)*

End of Act I

ACT II

Scene One

(A week later. A hill on the edge of town. **RACHEL** *and* **ABHI** *are climbing.)*

ABHI. But don't you want to at least *meet* the person who will be half of your child's genetic makeup?

RACHEL. Does this topic have to dominate our every conversation? I never would have told you if I'd known you were going to hound me about it for the next millennium.

ABHI. I am sorry. I am simply...curious, that is all.

RACHEL. I understand. It must be scary to learn that your whole gender is becoming obsolete.

ABHI. Obsolete?

RACHEL. That's the fear, isn't it? That we won't need you any more?

ABHI. I don't know. I never thought about it.

RACHEL. Not consciously.

ABHI. You mean –

RACHEL. I mean you're obsessed!

ABHI. I'm not –

RACHEL. Now who's in denial? *(stops to breathe)* How much farther do we have to climb?

ABHI. Just a few more minutes.

RACHEL. You said that half an hour ago.

ABHI. I promise you, it is worth it. The view from the top is exquisite.

RACHEL. Okay, but if I die of heatstroke I'm suing your ass.

ABHI. Suing my –

RACHEL. Never mind. And yes. For your information, I did want a friend to donate, at first.

ABHI. To donate what?

(**RACHEL** *looks at him.*)

Oh.

RACHEL. My friend Mike and his wife were doing their medical residencies at San Francisco General Hospital. So one day I went over there on their lunch break to talk it over with them.

(**MIKE** *and* **TERI** *appear on the other side of the stage. They are two peas in a pod, dressed in lab coats and matching glasses, eating sandwiches and drinking diet sodas.*)

MIKE. *(serious, even moved)* You're asking me to be the father of your child?

ABHI. He said no?

RACHEL. *(to both of them)* Not exactly.

ABHI, MIKE, & TERI. What do you mean?

RACHEL. *(moving toward* **MIKE***)* What I mean is, I'd love for you to know the child, and you could be involved as like, a friendly uncle – and aunt – if you wanted to, but you wouldn't be the father. You'd be the donor.

MIKE. What about financial responsibility?

TERI. What if something happened to you?

ABHI. Who would care for the child?

RACHEL. I –

MIKE. I'm not saying I'm not open to it...

RACHEL. We'd sign a contract ahead of time. I'd designate someone in my family as legal guardian if anything should happen to me. You'd have no legal rights or obligations.

TERI. Is there *precedent* for that?

RACHEL. Yes! You just have to make it clear right out the gate that it's a donor relationship. You go through a doctor; there's no intercourse involved –

MIKE. *(playful)* Wait a minute, you mean this doesn't involve
    sex?

RACHEL. *(smiles)* We could negotiate that.

TERI. Hey! I'm right here!

ABHI. So his wife objected.

RACHEL. *(to ABHI)* They had some concerns.

> *(The following lines, to the end of the* MIKE *and* TERI
> *section, should come with increasing rapidity, interrupt-*
> *ing and overlapping each other)*

TERI. Would you have the child baptized?

RACHEL. Of course not – I'm Jewish!

TERI. Because if Mike's parents found out they had a
    grandchild who wasn't baptized…

MIKE. Which school will you send him to?

TERI. …they would *freak*.

MIKE. Private school is expensive, you know.

RACHEL. What's wrong with public school?

MIKE. In your neighborhood?!

TERI. They are *serious* Catholics.

MIKE. No child of mine is getting left behind.

> *(*RACHEL *holds up her hands to stop them. To* ABHI*)*

RACHEL. We decided to table that idea.

ABHI. So you went to the…bank?

RACHEL. The sperm bank, yes. With my friend, the one I
    made the pact with. You pick your donor out of this
    huge catalog. We thought it would be fun to choose
    the same one, so our children would be biological sib-
    lings. We were having some trouble deciding, so they
    let us take the catalog home.

> *(*ANJALI *appears in a pool of light, lying on their bed-*
> *room floor.* ANJALI *and* RACHEL*'s affection for each*
> *other should be evident throughout their bantering.)*

ANJALI. This one sounds interesting. Doctor of Theology
    and Master's in computer science.

RACHEL. Hm. Yeah. Blonde, though.

ANJALI. So?

RACHEL. Don't like blondes. Don't want a pasty child. Oooh: Irish, Japanese, and Russian. How's that for a combo? Six-two, one eighty-five...

ANJALI. Mother diabetes, father heart disease, uncle alcoholism.

RACHEL. Ouch. *(sighs)* Too bad. *(flipping through)* Blonde, blonde, red... Okay. Here we go. Dark curly hair, olive skin. Six feet, one-eighty, Nicaraguan/Mexican/Italian. Yum yum.

ANJALI. Do you think you objectify men of color?

RACHEL. I objectify all men. Some objects just happen to look better than others.

ANJALI. Seriously, Rachel –

RACHEL. Here comes the lecture.

ANJALI. You call yourself progressive, but you refuse to examine your own unconscious –

RACHEL. It's an aesthetic preference! Who am I exploiting if I happen to think dark is prettier than light? It's not like the Swedish are out front picketing for equal access to my womb.

ANJALI. *(cracking up in spite of herself)* God, you're obnoxious. You should have been a lawyer.

RACHEL. I know. That's why you love me. Now, back to our Latin lover...

ANJALI. Rachel!

RACHEL. Oh forget it, look at this.

ANJALI. What?

RACHEL. 2.0 GPA.

ANJALI. So he's not academic, big deal.

RACHEL. He spelled motivation with an "s-h."

ANJALI. Maybe English isn't his first language.

RACHEL. He was born in Cleveland.

ANJALI. *(groans)* God, Rachel, there's always something.

RACHEL. You've ruled out as many as I have.

ANJALI. *(humorously defensive)* I have not.

RACHEL. Have too.

ANJALI. *(laughing)* Have not!

RACHEL. Have too.

ANJALI. *(counting on her fingers)* You didn't want 236 because he was too skinny. You didn't want 337 because he was too fat.

(Lights cross-fade over the rest of ANJALI's line.)

You didn't want 463 because his great-uncle had cancer. You didn't want 582 because he had acne as a teenager!

RACHEL. *(to ABHI)* We decided we'd each pick our own sperm.

ABHI. *(bursts out)* It is simply not natural!

RACHEL. What?

ABHI. For a woman to have a child without a man!

RACHEL. See? What did I tell you? Obsessed.

ABHI. But you *must* know somewhere within you that this is not the right path.

RACHEL. *(bridling)* No, I don't know that! I don't know that at all! This isn't a decision of the mind, Abhi. I didn't sit down one day and say, "Hmm, I think it would be a good idea to have a baby alone." No! The urge is physical. It tugs at my body like gravity. How can you say that's not natural?

ABHI. *(pause)* You truly feel it that way? In your body? Is it really that...fundamental?

RACHEL. Yes. I feel as if a child is out there, somewhere, calling to me. And I ask it: "What do you want to come here for? And why do you want *me*? I'm hardly a catch." But it does. It insists. It wants me.

ABHI. So what is stopping you from going forward?

RACHEL. Nothing – I told you! I got this job, so I had to –

ABHI. Rachel.

RACHEL. What?

ABHI. What was that word you just used? "Denial?"

RACHEL. There you go again! You have this way of turning things around.

ABHI. And you have this way of avoiding the truth.

RACHEL. I'm not –

ABHI. What are you denying?

RACHEL. Nothing.

ABHI. Nothing?

RACHEL. Nothing!

ABHI. Rachel.

RACHEL. Okay, then! Fear!

ABHI. Of what?

RACHEL. That I can't do it.

ABHI. That you can't have children?

RACHEL. That I can't *be a mother.*

ABHI. That makes no sense.

RACHEL. That I'm not grown up enough to handle it. That I'd freak out, run away, end up roaming the streets in my nightgown ranting at lampposts while my baby's at home in week-old diapers screaming for food. Or worse, that I'd lose it completely and do some horrible evil thing, like those women you read about in the papers, who… *(She can't complete the thought.)*

ABHI. You think you would –

RACHEL. No! I don't *think* I would, of course not, but people do, they do things! They abandon children, they hurt them, they neglect them. I'm sure they don't plan to do those things, but what if…what if I can't…?

ABHI. *(puts a hand on her arm, awkwardly)* These are only phantoms, Rachel. You would never hurt a child.

RACHEL. How do you know?

ABHI. I know.

RACHEL. Thank you.

ABHI. *(gesturing in front of them)* Look.

(They have been standing on the crest of the hill for a while, but they were so absorbed in conversation that they did not realize it. Now **RACHEL** *looks at the view.)*

RACHEL. Oh. Agra.

(They pause for a long moment, taking it in.)

ABHI. There it is. All of it. Rickshaws and automobiles, grapevines and electrical wires, sandstone palaces and plastic tents. And there, flowing through it all, the Yamuna River, powerful and serenely indifferent.

RACHEL. Indifferent?

ABHI. That is the key to her serenity. She is unmoved by our suffering. This is not cruelty, mind you. It is only that, to her, our human struggles are as light as insects, too small to pierce the surface. She has seen so many like us come and go.

RACHEL. Lucky her.

ABHI. Rachel. This fear you spoke of. Are you sure that is the only thing standing in your way?

RACHEL. Oh…and I guess there's…there's probably still some tiny stupid part of me that thinks Prince Charming is going to waltz in at the eleventh hour and save me from myself.

ABHI. And if such a man were to appear? Would you accept him?

(They look at each other. **RACHEL** *leans slightly toward him, and they kiss. After a moment, he pulls away.)*

ABHI. I'm sorry. I'm so sorry. Forgive me.

RACHEL. For what?

ABHI. You are a guest of my family. I should not have taken advantage.

RACHEL. Taken advantage? Hello! I kissed you.

ABHI. Then you…You're not…You don't mind?

RACHEL. I don't. Not at all.

(She smiles at him. They kiss again for a long moment as the lights begin to fade.)

Scene Two

(The next day. **RACHEL** *and* **ANJALI** *are on the telephone in their respective bedrooms.)*

ANJALI. So you're having fun?

RACHEL. Oh, yeah. The time is just flying by. Can you believe it's been three weeks already?

ANJALI. I'm afraid the clock's creeping a bit more slowly on this end. How's the heat?

RACHEL. Oh, you know, it's not so bad, as long as you don't try to *do* anything between, like, eleven and four...

ANJALI. Which monuments have you been to?

RACHEL. Oh, God, everything. The Taj, the Baby Taj, Fatehpur Sikri, Akbar's Mausoleum, Mariyam's Tomb... Tomorrow we're going to the Red Fort.

ANJALI. We?

RACHEL. Your cousin Abhi's been showing me around.

ANJALI. Oh, you managed to draw him out of his shell.

RACHEL. *(evasive)* Yeah. Nice guy. *(short pause)* Anyway, how are you?

ANJALI. Fine. *(pause)* I've –

RACHEL. *(overlapping)* That's great, sweetie; I'm glad everything's going well. Listen, I've gotta run. I'm supposed to file one of these columns in an hour and I've barely started it. I'll talk to you next week, okay?

(Lights down on **RACHEL**. **ANJALI** *sits for a moment, then slowly hangs up the phone. She puts a hand on her abdomen. Lights fade.)*

Scene Three

*(Two days later. The Sharmas' living room. **RACHEL** sits on the couch. There are two glasses on the coffee table. **CHANDRA** enters, dancing. She holds a bottle of dark rum. **CHANDRA**'s attitude in this scene is straightforwardly curious rather than flirtatious.)*

RACHEL. I would not have pegged you for a drinker, Chandra.

CHANDRA. I don't drink.

RACHEL. What's that in your hand?

CHANDRA. Only on special occasions.

RACHEL. What's the occasion?

CHANDRA. My husband is away tonight…And it is my last night of freedom.

RACHEL. What do you mean?

*(**CHANDRA** pours a glass of rum and hands it to **RACHEL**.)*

CHANDRA. My mother-in-law returns tomorrow.

RACHEL. Oooooh. I was wondering when she was going to turn up. Should I be afraid?

CHANDRA. No, you? You are her guest. Not her daughter-in-law. But let's not think about her tonight. *(turns up music)* Come on. Let's dance!

*(Pulls **RACHEL** up. They dance. **CHANDRA** moves in very close, making **RACHEL** suddenly nervous.)*

RACHEL. God, it's *hot!*

CHANDRA. Shall I pour some water on you?

RACHEL. Sure.

CHANDRA. Remove your clothes.

RACHEL. Excuse me?

CHANDRA. *(matter-of-fact)* Remove your clothes.

RACHEL. That's okay, I don't mind getting them wet.

CHANDRA. Sachi and Osho are asleep. There is no one else at home.

RACHEL. It's okay.

CHANDRA. Come on. I am curious.

RACHEL. About what?

CHANDRA. I want to see your body.

RACHEL. *(laughing)* You're drunk.

CHANDRA. Why not? The curtains are drawn.

RACHEL. No.

CHANDRA. Yes. *(picks up a glass and flings water on* **RACHEL***)*

RACHEL. No! *(picks up the other glass and flings water at* **CHANDRA***)*

CHANDRA. *Eh!* This is a new sari! *(flings the rest of her glass)*

RACHEL. You started it! *(picks up the pitcher)*

CHANDRA. No! *(tries to calm her down)* Please. This is not necessary. Truce.

RACHEL. Truce?

CHANDRA. Truce.

RACHEL. Okay. Truce.

*(***RACHEL*** puts down the pitcher. ***CHANDRA*** picks it up and flings the entire contents on ***RACHEL***. ***RACHEL*** shrieks.)*

CHANDRA. Ha! Now you *must* remove your clothes. You will spoil my furniture!

RACHEL. You're out of your mind!

CHANDRA. *(pouting)* The other girls showed me their bodies. Trinity's body was so slim and strong. She told me she sees other girls' bodies all the time, in the locker room at the swimming pool. She said in your country it is just normal.

RACHEL. Well yes, but everyone's changing. No one's just sitting there watching. I'll tell you what. If you want to take off your clothes, I'll take mine off too, and we can have a naked conversation.

CHANDRA. Oh, no, I cannot show you my body. I have given birth – I have a scar! My body is not smooth and pretty like yours.

RACHEL. Chandra, do you think it's possible that you're bisexual?

CHANDRA. Bisexual?

RACHEL. Attracted to both women and men?

CHANDRA. *(giggles)* Oh, no! How can I be bisexual? I can barely tolerate my husband!

RACHEL. Uh-huh. *(pause)* I'll just duck into the other room and change, okay? You stay there. Stay right there.

(RACHEL goes into the other room.)

CHANDRA. *(calling to her)* Trinity was like this, bisexual. When she left she asked if she could kiss me. "On the cheek?" I asked. "No," she said, "on the lips." First I said yes, but then I said no, only on the cheek. *(pause)* What about Anjali? Do you think she is like this?

RACHEL. *(from offstage)* Anjali, bisexual? *(smiling inwardly)* No. I don't think so.

CHANDRA. Are you sure? I have seen her pictures in America! She dresses like a boy. *(pause)* Trinity likes sex to be rough, she told me. She likes to be tied with ropes. Do you like that?

RACHEL. No comment!

CHANDRA. I cannot bear to be rough. Only the very most gentle. And even that I can scarcely bear. Now I have not wanted sex for some six months, since I scraped my knee. He goes to other women, now. I can tell from the way he walks afterwards, like some kind of American cowboy who just "roped a steer."

(RACHEL emerges, dressed.)

RACHEL. Does it bother you that he sleeps with other women?

CHANDRA. I thought it would, but as long as he keeps it out of the house, I actually find it a relief. Of course I could never tell him that. He believes he is keeping it a secret. If he knew that I knew about it and did not mind, it would hurt his pride terribly.

RACHEL. *(pause)* Do you love him?

CHANDRA. *(Lighting up. with feeling)* Of course I love him. He is my husband! And he is kind to me. When I was pregnant with Sachi, there were complications. The doctor wanted to perform a Caesarian, but my husband would not permit it. He said, "My wife is so tender, she cannot stand even a small scratch on her arm. How can she bear to be cut open?" But the doctor said that without an operation he could not save both. Either I or the baby must die. My husband said, "Then save my wife." *(pause)* Then my mother-in-law intervened. She said, "If it is possible to save both, then you must do so." And so the operation was performed.

RACHEL. Was it okay?

CHANDRA. Okay? It was terrible. For weeks I could hardly leave my bed. But we have my daughter.

RACHEL. She's adorable.

CHANDRA. I hope she will behave better than her brother. He is soooo naughty. He will drive me mad.

RACHEL. *(cautious)* Did you *want* to be a mother?

CHANDRA. Never. When I married, I prayed secretly that I would not be able to bear children. I wanted that teaching post, and I knew that if I had children, Mrs. Sharma would keep me at home until they were grown.

RACHEL. So you regret having them.

CHANDRA. Regret? No. I regret abandoning my studies, but I cannot regret giving birth to those two. It's true I would not have chosen it, but now that they are here, I cannot imagine life without them. Even that impudent Osho is like a part of my own self. They come into this world with only their hunger, knowing nothing, not even that the little hands flapping in front of their faces are their own. They depend on you completely, so you cannot help but love them completely.

RACHEL. Yeah. Sometimes I wish I'd just get pregnant by accident, because I know I'd be crazy about the child once it was here.

CHANDRA. How can you wish for that? The humiliation would be intolerable.

RACHEL. It's different...

CHANDRA. In your country. It must be. It's funny; here we wish only for a few more options, and you, with all the options in the world...

RACHEL. ...can't make up my mind? It is sort of ironic, now that you mention it. *(pause)* So are you planning for number three yet?

CHANDRA. Oh, no! Two is enough. I will never go through that again.

RACHEL. Arustu's okay with that?

CHANDRA. He agrees. His mother does not like it, but on this one matter he stands up to her. He is not a bad man. Only the sex; that I cannot bear.

Scene Four

*(The hallway outside Mrs. Vasudhara Sharma's bed-
room.* SUNITA *passes, carrying a pile of laundry. As
she crosses,* RACHEL *enters from offstage, and* ARUSTU
*emerges from inside the room, closing the door quietly
behind him.)*

RACHEL. *(to* ARUSTU*)* Is she awake?

ARUSTU. *(nods)* She has been asking for you.

*(*RACHEL *knocks timidly.)*

MRS. SHARMA. Come in.

*(*RACHEL *crosses to the bedroom.* SUNITA *starts to exit.*
ARUSTU *looks behind him to make sure that* RACHEL *is
not watching, then puts his arm around* SUNITA*. She
cringes, ducking her head. They exit together.)*

Scene Five

(Mrs. Sharma's bedroom)

MRS. SHARMA. Please, come closer. Feel free.

(RACHEL enters.)

RACHEL. Namaste.

MRS. SHARMA. Namaskar.

RACHEL. Have you recovered from your journey?

MRS. SHARMA. At my age one never recovers from anything.

RACHEL. I want to thank you so much for opening your home to me.

MRS. SHARMA. Nothing to thank. Anjali's friends are our friends. Has my daughter-in-law treated you well?

RACHEL. Everyone's been extremely kind. You have a wonderful family.

MRS. SHARMA. How old?

RACHEL. Excuse me?

MRS. SHARMA. You. How old?

RACHEL. *(sighs)* Thirty-seven.

MRS. SHARMA. You are married?

RACHEL. No.

MRS. SHARMA. Traveling alone?

RACHEL. Yes. Traveling and writing.

MRS. SHARMA. Good. That is the best life for a woman. No obligations.

RACHEL. You're the first person I've met here who's said that.

MRS. SHARMA. I understand that my granddaughter Anjali is not inclined to marry either.

RACHEL. I –

MRS. SHARMA. Has she involved herself with an American boy?

RACHEL. *(shaking her head)*

MRS. SHARMA. Or perhaps with an American girl?

(**RACHEL** *stares.*)

You are surprised?

RACHEL. I, well, yes.

MRS. SHARMA. That girl has been dropping hints for the past fifteen years! Does she think her family is blind? I am old, not stupid. These things are not unknown to me. I suspect my daughter-in-law would have the same tastes if given the chance to indulge them.

(**RACHEL** *gapes at her.*)

Again you are surprised. There can be no secrets in this house. For my son, of course, I would prefer she were otherwise. It drives him to impropriety. But they are no more unhappy than most. He adores her, and she tolerates him. They made their choices and they accept the consequences. I wish Anjali would do the same.

RACHEL. That she…

MRS. SHARMA. That she would choose her path and live it! Stop hiding herself away like a coward, as though a harsh word would strike her to the ground. What does she think would happen if she told her family the truth?

RACHEL. I suppose she's afraid you wouldn't accept her.

MRS. SHARMA. But that is just the point! I must accept her. This world is not tailored to my fancies. I would *prefer* that Anjali's mother were alive, and that both mother and daughter were living in Agra, but that is not the case. I accept what is so and get on with things, as my mother did before me, as my daughters and daughters-in-law must also do. That is what it means to be a woman. But you know this already.

RACHEL. Do I?

MRS. SHARMA. Of course! You are a smart girl. You travel the world as a guest, free of all responsibility. *(bellows)* Chandra! Chandra! Chai! *(pause)* You see how smart you are? No husband, no mother-in-law. *(smiles)*

Scene Six

(The bedroom at the Sharma house. **RACHEL** *is on the phone.)*

ANJALI. *(voiceover)* Hi, this is Anjali Narayan. Please leave me an intriguing message.

(A beep sounds.)

RACHEL. Okay, Anj, now you're worrying me. What's up? You haven't returned my last three calls. Could you at least shoot me an email or something, even if it's just to say that you're totally pissed off at me and you don't want to talk? Thanks. I love you. Talk to you soon.

Scene Seven

(The Agra Fort. Music. The narration at the beginning of the scene is enacted in a stylized fashion, perhaps with puppets. **ABHI** *and* **RACHEL** *stand in shadows. Throughout this scene, they behave in a giddy, lovestruck way.)*

ABHI. Shah Jahan and Mumtaz Mahal had four sons. The boys were bitter rivals, almost from birth. As children, they imitated the scheming machinations they saw in the court with their own shifting alliances. Often, three of them joined forces to torment their unlucky brother, locking him into a stifling tower or dungeon, where he would howl for hours until he was released.

(A **BOY** *appears in a pool of light, wailing and pounding melodramatically on an imaginary door while echoing laughter is heard.)*

In 1657, Shah Jahan fell ill. His sons, now middle-aged, fought desperately for the throne. Shah Jahan had hoped to pass on the throne to his eldest son, Dara Shukoh, but Dara was an artist and intellectual, and no match for his wily younger brother Aurangzeb. Aurangzeb won the allegiance of the army, locked his father in the Agra Fort - in this very tower - and proclaimed himself Emperor. Shah Jahan lived in this tower for seven years. He died looking out that window, gazing across the Yamuna River at his most magnificent creation and dreaming of his beloved wife.

(Lights fade up on **ABHI** *and* **RACHEL**.*)*

RACHEL. Poor Shah Jahan.

(She puts a hand to **ABHI** *'s face.)*

ABHI. He probably deserved it.

RACHEL. *(surprised)* What?

ABHI. He was a brutal man.

RACHEL. I thought he was your hero.

ABHI. That doesn't mean that I am blind to his faults.

(They kiss. A tourist enters. **ABHI** *abruptly breaks away.)*

RACHEL. What? *(***ABHI** *indicates the other person)* Oh.

ABHI. *(straightens himself out)* Shah Jahan killed his own brothers, you know.

RACHEL. He did?

ABHI. Mm hm. As soon as he ascended the throne. Of course, they would most likely have killed him if he hadn't.

RACHEL. So much for brotherly love. *(pause)* It's a sad end, though, to be locked away by your own son. We expect our children to love us, but who knows? There's certainly no guarantee.

(The other tourist exits.)

ABHI. They will love you.

RACHEL. You always say these things. How do you know?

ABHI. I know.

*(***RACHEL** *smiles. They kiss some more. Again* **ABHI** *breaks off.)*

RACHEL. *(laughing)* What?

ABHI. I thought someone was there.

RACHEL. You're not used to kissing in public.

ABHI. *(laughs)* We do not even hold hands in public. I am not used to kissing at all.

RACHEL. You could've fooled me.

ABHI. What do you mean?

RACHEL. I mean…you kiss like a pro.

ABHI. *(Laughs, embarrassed. Pause.)* Really?

RACHEL. Mm hm. Like you've been doing it all your life.

(They kiss.)

ABHI. I am so grateful to you, Rachel.

RACHEL. Why?

ABHI. For lifting me from my shyness.

RACHEL. Oh Abhi, why should you be shy? You're so brilliant and charming and…eloquent. And so romantic.

ABHI. I am romantic, it is true, but until now all the romance has taken place inside my head. I've been living in these stories. I share them with my students, of course, but they are bored by them. Or perhaps it was I who had grown bored. Sharing them with you has made them fresh. *(Pause. Deep breath.)* Rachel.

RACHEL. Yes?

ABHI. I'd like to invite you to meet my mother.

RACHEL. Oh! I...

ABHI. If you don't want to...

RACHEL. No, I'd love to, it's just...

ABHI. What?

RACHEL. Nothing. *(Pause. Decisive)* Nothing. I'd love to.

ABHI. Wonderful. How about dinner Saturday night?

Scene Eight

(ANJALI and RACHEL are on the phone. RACHEL is in the usual location. ANJALI is in a hospital corridor, dressed in a hospital gown. She is visibly exhausted. Hospital sounds in the background.)

ANJALI. It's me, Rachel.

RACHEL. Anjali! Thank God! Didn't you get my messages?

ANJALI. Yes, but –

RACHEL. How come you didn't call me back sooner? I was afraid –

ANJALI. I didn't call because I'm in the hospital.

RACHEL. Why? What? Is it the baby?

ANJALI. She was born four days ago, by emergency Caesarian.

RACHEL. Oh my God. Is she okay?

ANJALI. Okay? No. You don't come out "okay" at twenty-four weeks. She's alive.

RACHEL. But is she... Will she...

ANJALI. She could be fine, eventually, or there could be long-term consequences. *If* she... *(She can't finish the sentence.)*

RACHEL. Oh sweetheart. Oh my God. How? What happened?

ANJALI. I got preeclampsia.

RACHEL. Pre – What's that?

ANJALI. It's... One morning my hands were so bloated I couldn't get my rings on. I looked in the mirror and my face was all blotchy and swollen. It turned out my blood pressure was 200 over 110. They kept me in the hospital on bed rest, but then the placenta separated and they had to take her out.

RACHEL. Oh Anj. I'm so sorry.

ANJALI. I barely got to look at her before they took her away. They have her in a special room with the other... If you could *see* them, Rachel, the babies. All alone in their glass bubbles, with tubes and needles sticking into them. They look like little...red...*frogs*. The first time I touched her, all these alarms went off. Her heart had stopped beating. The nurse had to rub her chest to start it up again.

RACHEL. Oh my God. I'm so sorry.

ANJALI. *(fighting for control)* I wish I could hold her.

RACHEL. Oh sweetheart, I'm so... *(pause)* I'll come home right away. I'll get on the next plane.

ANJALI. No, you finish up what you're doing. You're coming home Monday anyway, right?

RACHEL. Monday. Yes! Right. Monday.

ANJALI. Good.

RACHEL. Monday, of course. You need me...don't you?

ANJALI. You're asking...?

RACHEL. No. It's just... You shouldn't be alone at a time like this, right?

ANJALI. Is that a question?

RACHEL. I'm just thinking out –

ANJALI. *(with dawning incredulity)* You were going to extend your trip, weren't you? What is it this time? Another "amazing" assignment? A man?

RACHEL. No! I just – I wanted to be sure that you –

ANJALI. Sure that I what? That I'm completely desperate? That I can't survive without you?

RACHEL. No, I –

ANJALI. Just...do what's best for you, okay Rachel? You always do anyway.

(She hangs up. Lights out on ANJALI.*)*

RACHEL. Wait, that's not – Anjali? *(pause)* Anjali?
*(*RACHEL *holds the phone a moment, then hangs up.)*
Oh God.

(lights out)

Scene Nine

(A street corner. **ABHI** *and* **RACHEL** *are waiting for a bus.)*

ABHI. *(excited)* She looks imposing, but in fact she is quite timid. People think she does not like them, because she has a vision problem which causes her to squint, so it appears that she is frowning. But you mustn't worry. She will love you immediately. She is very Western in her thinking, actually. Although her own marriage was quite traditional, she is very supportive of women having their own careers. *(Pause. Notices that* **RACHEL** *appears distracted.)* What is wrong?

RACHEL. Nothing.

ABHI. What?

RACHEL. Nothing. We'll talk after dinner. *(pause)* When does the bus come?

ABHI. Soon. *(pause)* What is the matter, Rachel? If you have something to tell me, perhaps you should do it now. Otherwise your mind will be preoccupied and you will not enjoy the evening.

RACHEL. I'm okay.

ABHI. All right, then *my* mind will be preoccupied and I will not enjoy the evening.

RACHEL. This isn't exactly private.

ABHI. There is a quiet alley just here.

RACHEL. What about the bus?

ABHI. We have time.

(They walk for a moment in silence, then stop. **ABHI** *looks at* **RACHEL** *expectantly.)*

RACHEL. Don't look at me like that.

(He turns away.)

Okay, that's worse.

(He turns back and looks at her. Pause. She blurts.)

I have to go, Abhi.

ABHI. To go? Where?

RACHEL. Home. Back to the U.S.

ABHI. I thought you changed your ticket.

RACHEL. I had to change it back again.

ABHI. Why?

RACHEL. My friend…Lisa. Something's come up. An emergency.

ABHI. What is it?

RACHEL. I can't say.

ABHI. You can't say?

RACHEL. No. It's…confidential. *(pause)* Believe me, leaving is the last thing I want to do right now. I'd much rather stay here with you. But…she needs me.

ABHI. When will you go?

RACHEL. Monday.

ABHI. That's the day after tomorrow!

RACHEL. I know.

ABHI. And when will you return?

RACHEL. I don't know.

ABHI. A week? A month?

RACHEL. *(evasive)* Something like that.

ABHI. Something –

RACHEL. I'm not sure. It could be a while.

> *(Pause. He looks at her.)*

The situation's ongoing, okay? It's out of my control.

ABHI. I see.

RACHEL. *(soft and almost flirtatious, thinking she can make it okay)* I'll miss you.

ABHI. So that's it, huh? "Had a nice time, see you later?"

RACHEL. I told you, I don't *want* to go. I have to.

ABHI. *(Softly. Incredulous)* I am a fool.

RACHEL. Excuse me?

ABHI. I am a complete and total fool. I am the biggest idiot ever to walk the face of the earth.

RACHEL. What are you talking about?

ABHI. I almost introduced you to my mother! Thank God I discovered the truth in time.

RACHEL. What truth?

ABHI. What truth? There's usually only one. You, Rachel. What you are.

RACHEL. *What?*

ABHI. You *use* people. Men. You get what you want from them, and then when they begin to care for you, you invent an excuse to run away. You told me yourself, only I was too stupid to listen.

(In the following lines, ABHI's thoughts come rapidly, overlapping RACHEL's interjections.)

RACHEL. That's not –

ABHI. There is no emergency, is there?

RACHEL. Of course –

ABHI. There's no "Lisa!"

RACHEL. There…I…

ABHI. You got what you came for and now you're clearing out.

RACHEL. I –

ABHI. I really spiced up your travel essays, didn't I? Nothing like an exotic romance to add some "local color."

RACHEL. Oh, Abhi, that's not – No! The time I spent with you has been… It's been the most beautiful, the most amazing –

ABHI. Please! No more lies.

(Sound of the bus arriving. ABHI starts to leave, but his manners won't permit it. He returns, disgusted.)

Come. I must return you to my cousin's home.

(He starts away again, sees she is not following.)

Come!

(He turns and continues walking. RACHEL slowly follows, at a slight distance. Lights out.)

Scene Ten

*(The Sharmas' living room. **CHANDRA** chasing **OSHO** around, quizzing him on English spelling in the study. **RACHEL** sits in the living room with a book, staring into space.)*

CHANDRA. Hammer.

OSHO. H-A-M-M-E-R.

CHANDRA. Plane.

OSHO. P-L-A-N-E. *(imploring)* Please can't I go play now?

CHANDRA. Eleven words to go. Exit!

OSHO. *(running off)* E-X-I-T!

CHANDRA. *Eh! Vaapas aao, abhi, isi waqt!* Come back here, naughty boy! *(She storms into the living room.)* That is the end of it. I am sending him to boarding school. He cannot sit still for five minutes!

RACHEL. He's six years old.

CHANDRA. When I was six years old, I was reading the classics. I knew my multiplication tables by heart.

RACHEL. Maybe he's not like you.

CHANDRA. But he can be. He simply does not try.

*(**ARUSTU** enters.)*

ARUSTU. What have you done to the boy? He is hiding under his bed.

CHANDRA. I have done nothing to him. It is he who has done to me. He has made me an old woman before my time. I told him I will take him to the railway station and put him on the next train to Delhi. He can see how he enjoys living in my father's house.

ARUSTU. No wonder the boy is frightened. *(noticing **RACHEL**)* Rachel! Rumor has it you plan to leave us tomorrow.

RACHEL. It's true, I'm afraid.

ARUSTU. Has India answered your questions for you?

CHANDRA. I can tell you the answer right now. Do not have children. They will torture you when you are young and abandon you when you grow old.

ARUSTU. And what about Abhiji?

RACHEL. *(trying for lightness)* What about him?

ARUSTU. I thought you two were getting along sooo nicely.

RACHEL. He's a lovely guy.

ARUSTU. "A lovely guy?" And yet you will desert him, just like that?

RACHEL. I don't have a choice.

ARUSTU. No choice? I thought to you Americans everything is a choice. "We create our own reality." Isn't that your philosophy?

RACHEL. Fine. It's a choice I have to make, okay?

ARUSTU. I only –

CHANDRA. *(pointed)* Arustuji, I am so hungry. Will you please go to the kitchen and ask Deepa what time the dinner will be ready?

*(**ARUSTU** glares at **CHANDRA**, who glares back. He exits, perplexed.)*

RACHEL. Who's Deepa?

CHANDRA. Our new girl. We had to let the other one go.

RACHEL. Sunita?

CHANDRA. As I told you, Arustu may do as he likes, *as long as he keeps it out of this house.*

RACHEL. *(shocked)* No.

CHANDRA. *(shrugging it off)* A shame. She was a good worker. Do not let my husband bother you about Abhi. He will recover. Arustu does not like to see his cousin sad, that is all.

RACHEL. He saw him?

CHANDRA. He tried. Since you came home so early last night, Arustu went to Abhi's house today to find out what happened. Abhi's mother told him that Abhi had not come out of his room the whole day long.

*(**RACHEL** is completely shocked by this news. **CHANDRA** continues, unaware.)*

CHANDRA. *(cont.)* These men and their dramas. They call us irrational, but in fact it is they who are ruled by their overactive imaginations! What did Abhi think, that you had fallen in love with him? That you would change your entire life around over some little flirtation?

But Rachel, I must tell you quickly. I have written to the university.

RACHEL. The university?

CHANDRA. I saw a notice for a teaching post, in chemistry. Remember you asked me, "Why does Mrs. Sharma keep you in the house, when she goes out into the world and works?" I could not stop thinking of it. I can work while Osho is in school, and Arustu can care for Sachi while I am away. He will not like it, but he will agree. Besides, since you are here, he is frightened that I will leave him. I said to him the other night, "If Rachel can raise her child without a man, don't think that I cannot."

RACHEL. *(startled)* How did you –

CHANDRA. There are no secrets in this house. *(lowering voice further)* Only I must keep my plans from my mother-in-law until the matter is resolved. She has connections at the university. She could easily spoil my chances.

MRS. SHARMA. *(from offstage)* Chandra! What is all this whispering about?*

CHANDRA. Nothing, Ammaji. Only, I thought you were napping. I did not wish to disturb you.

(ARUSTU enters, pushing OSHO ahead of him.)

ARUSTU. *(to CHANDRA)* The boy has something to say to you.

CHANDRA. And what might that be?

OSHO. I am sorry, Mummy.

CHANDRA. I will let it go this one time only. But from now on, you must learn to concentrate. Now give your mother a kiss.

---

* If Chandra and Mrs. Sharma are doubled, Mrs. Sharma's offstage shout would need to be on tape or performed by another actor.

ARUSTU. And so, with a little "I am sorry," peace is restored to the happy family.

CHANDRA. So why am I never hearing these words from you?

ARUSTU. I am sorry? I did not hear you. Come, dinner is ready.

*(***ARUSTU***, ***CHANDRA***, and* ***OSHO*** *exit.* ***RACHEL*** *watches them, then starts to cry. Lights dim to a spot, music signals the passage of time. Determinedly,* ***RACHEL*** *gets up and crosses downstage. She picks up the phone, dials.* ***ABHI*** *appears on the other side of the stage in pajamas, sleepily rubbing his eyes. He picks up the phone.)*

ABHI. Hello?

RACHEL. Abhi? It's Rachel.

(lights out)

Scene Eleven

(The Baby Taj. **RACHEL** *enters, tentatively.* **ABHI** *enters from the opposite side. Their lines in the first part of the scene should come quickly, overlapping, until* **RACHEL** *says "please.")*

ABHI. Rachel.

RACHEL. There you are.

ABHI. Rachel. I am sorry.

RACHEL. Oh, Abhi, I'm so sorry.

ABHI. My conduct was inexcusable.

RACHEL. Oh, Abhi, *no.* It's all my fault.

ABHI. No. You have always been honest with me. At every moment. I simply heard what I wanted to hear.

RACHEL. No. You had a right to be angry. These last couple of days, I've had to do a lot of thinking. And I –

ABHI. It is all right. You don't have to explain.

RACHEL. I do have to! Please. *(Pause. Looks at him.)* I have hurt a lot of people in my life, Abhi. I didn't set out to hurt them, but I hurt them all the same. And every time it happened, I told myself it wasn't my fault. I never lied to anyone. All I did was to be myself and live my truth, and if someone got hurt along the way, there was nothing I could do about it.

But now I see that *not lying* is not enough. That that kind of honesty is just another great excuse for not taking responsibility. For not taking care. And we need to *take care.*

I owe you more than what I gave you, Abhi. Much more. At the very least, I owe you an explanation. And the reason I didn't tell you, the only reason I didn't...

ABHI. Your friend.

RACHEL. Yes. The one I made the pact with. I wanted to keep her confidence. Because she asked me to. She was afraid of what her family would think if they knew the truth.

RACHEL. *(cont.)* Abhi. You were right. There is no Lisa. There's only me...and Anjali.

ABHI. Anjali?

RACHEL. Yes. Your cousin Anjali gave birth to a daughter. Early. Very early. This is the baby that she and I, in some way, *conceived* together. And this baby, this human being, she may not live. And if she does live, she may have long-term problems, that require special care. And Anjali...She's alone. She hasn't told her family, as you know. She has other friends of course, but those friendships are casual, superficial. I am the only person she really trusts.

ABHI. Anjali. My God.

RACHEL. *(pause)* Abhi. The time I've spent with you has been free and joyous and magical beyond anything I can possibly express. But Anjali has come through for me again and again, through...oh, God, all kinds of, I can't even tell you...almost ten years! And she never... She never asks me for anything – I'm always the one who comes to her. And now I...I set this thing in motion. It was my idea. *(pause)* She is my dearest and truest friend. And even though it's not the *kind* of relationship the world considers worthy of building a life around – It is the deepest, most stable relationship I have ever known. If I don't come through for her now, how can I ever trust myself?

ABHI. I understand.

RACHEL. Do you? *(pause)* I look at you and I see a person for whom honesty and integrity are as basic as air. I've never known anyone like you, Abhi. You thrill me, and you inspire me, and God, you scare the hell out of me. Your eyes on me, even now, are so open and tender. They *unbind* me. It's like you see every stupid thing I've ever done and you forgive me for it. And I don't know if I'm ready for that.

ABHI. You are –

RACHEL. There's something else, too. I want a baby. More than anything in the world. I just can't wait anymore. All my life there's been so little I was sure of, but when I close my eyes and get past all the arguments and judgments and self-doubt, I am sure of this one thing. *(pause)* And...

ABHI. Shhhh... *(He puts a finger to her lips.)* No more words.

(He kisses her. They start kissing heavily. The courtyard opens up, and the historical characters move in around them, embracing in sensual stylized gestures. ABHI and RACHEL begin removing each others' clothes, gradually going from standing to kneeling.)

RACHEL. Are you sure we should be doing this?

ABHI. Yes.

RACHEL. Because I thought...I thought you were waiting... for marriage, or...

ABHI. I was.

RACHEL. But then we shouldn't.

ABHI. We should.

RACHEL. But why? Why me?

ABHI. Why you? *(pause)* Listen.

(Deep breath. He recites.)

I dreamed love as the Yamuna River
viscous, sultry, changing shape
I feared love as Himalayan winters'
brittle, fractured icy ache.

I found love in the ancient legends
Pure, heroic, carved in stone
And found that when the stories ended
Once again, I was alone.

For ages now my famished soul
Has wandered dusty, barren roads
A sadhu with a begging bowl
In search of what will make him whole

Until the day your sunburned face
Turned toward me with such candid grace
The heart within my heart awoke
And like a storm cloud, finally broke.

ABHI. *(cont.)* I wrote that for you the day we visited the Baby Taj, the first time you told me about your plan. I thought, then, that I would never have the courage to speak it to you, but that is only one of many things I never thought would come to pass.

(pause) I love you, Rachel. You jolted me back to my life. I am ready to live it.

(One by one the historical characters slip away.)

RACHEL. I love you, too. *(They laugh helplessly.)* Now what?

ABHI. Now you go back home and persuade that stubborn cousin of mine that her family's love did not die with her mother. That little girl deserves to know her relatives. If Anjali won't bring her to us, we may just have to come to her.

RACHEL. Really? Would you? You think you could –

ABHI. *(puts a finger to her lips)* Shhhh. Let us leave the future to discover itself. Now…I want to help you realize your dream.

*(They look at each other for a long moment, then continue their embrace. As the lights fade, music is heard, and **RACHEL**'s voice is heard in voiceover, as at the beginning.)*

RACHEL. *(voiceover)* What else can I offer you, my little traveler? Only my love, without condition or surrender. That, and the invitation to follow your own compass, wherever it may lead. It is a strange and beautiful world, and it will be better for your being in it. I hope you'll be glad you came.

(As the lights go to black, a baby's cry is heard.)

End of Play

OTHER TITLES AVAILABLE FROM SAMUEL FRENCH

LOVE PERSON

Aditi Brennan Kapil

Dramatic Comedy / 1m, 3f / Interior

Love Person is a four part love story in Sanskrit, ASL and English in which love transcends sexual orientation, physical attraction, and social structure and rests instead on the ways in which we communicate and how communication bonds or breaks us. The play is structured around four Sanskrit love poems that influence and reflect the journeys of the characters. Free, a deaf woman in a relationship with Maggie, accidentally falls into a deceptive email correspondence with her sister Vic's love interest Ram, a Sanskrit professor. Free and Ram discover a connection, based largely on an affinity between their two languages. As a result of the deception, Vic and Ram also begin to fall in love. Meanwhile Free and Maggie's relationship struggles to survive.

"Kapil's *Love Person* is a fascinating brew of emotion, wit and intellect that challenges its audience to reassess how the form of communication shapes understanding."
— *Lisa Brock, Minneapolis Star Tribune*

"Startling and evocative!
— *Michael Opperman, Twin Cities Daily Planet*

"Heart-pounding attraction, intense all-night conversations - Aditi Brennan Kapil's *Love Person* captures the giddiness of new love affairs. But the play is even more eloquently realistic about the wear and tear that time wreaks on relationships."
— *Nicole Estvanik, American Theatre Magazine, July 2008*

OTHER TITLES AVAILABLE FROM SAMUEL FRENCH

HUCK & HOLDEN

Rajiv Joseph

Full Length, Comedy / 3m, 2f / Unit set

Receiving rave reviews for both its New York and Los Angeles productions, Rajiv Joseph's *Huck & Holden* tells the story of Navin, an Indian college student who's fresh off the boat and trying to remain focused on his studies while the temptations of America and college life start beating down his door. When Navin falls for Michelle, a young African-American woman, he finds that his perceptions of the world begin to expand— and crumble. Called "…a comingof-age story with comedy, pathos, and a distinct emotional core," by offoffline.com, *Huck & Holden* is a romantic comedy that wrestles with cultural stereotypes, racism, The Kama Sutra, The Catcher in the Rye, and how losing our innocence doesn't always make us wiser.

"Joseph's writing has the smarts and sophistication to rip away stereotypes while revealing his characters' raw humanity. With simple storytelling, he deftly constructs Navin's coming-of-age story with comedy, pathos, and a distinct emotional core. This is theater at its finest, and theater that maters…. Everything in this highly polished production cries out for mention, but at the heart of it all is Joseph's taut, masterful script."
— *offoffonline.com*

"Rajiv Joseph's zesty comic fantasy *Huck & Holden*…bursts into utter hilarity."
— *Backstage.com*

"When Joseph hits, he knocks scenes out of the park, capturing that complicated area between elation and frustration that most people in their 20's seem to exclusively inhabit."
— *TalkinBroadway.com*

"A charming, goofy and frequently hilarious comedy of sex and romance."
— *BroadwayWorld.com*